TALES OF
AN 8-BIT
KITTEN
LOST IN THE NETHER

Published in French under the title *Un Chaton Qui S'est Perdu dans le Nether
Tome I* © 2017 by 404 éditions, an imprint of Édi8, Paris, France
Text © 2015 by Cube Kid, Illustration © 2016 by Vladimir "ZloyXP" Subbotin

Andrews McMeel Publishing
a division of Andrews McMeel Universal
1130 Walnut Street, Kansas City, Missouri 64106
www.andrewsmcmeel.com

22 23 24 25 26 SDB 10 9 8 7 6 5

ISBN: 978-1-4494-9447-6
Library of Congress Control Number: 2018932587

Made by:
King Yip (Dongguan) Printing & Packaging Factory Ltd.
Address and location of manufacturer:
Daning Administrative District, Humen Town
Dongguan Guangdong, China 523930
5th printing—6/10/22

TALES OF AN 8-BIT KITTEN

LOST IN THE NETHER

Illustrations by
Vladimir "ZloyXP" Subbotin

Andrews McMeel
PUBLISHING®

Eeebs was a **naughty little kitten. Very naughty,** in fact. He **never** listened to his mother.

She always told him: "Don't go too far into the forest, Son. It's **dangerous.** And if you ever see a purple light . . . run away. **Run** as fast as you can."

But Eeebs **loved** exploring the woods. He didn't think the forest was **dangerous at all.** No, it was an **interesting** place. Interesting and **mysterious.** He went there at least once a week—like today—along with his closest friends, **Tufty** and **Meowz.** The three of them had found a new meadow to play in. The meadow was filled with all kinds of **beautiful flowers.** They were **racing** to see who could pick the most.

Eeebs watched Meowz and Tufty **fight** over a lovely blue orchid. At last, Meowz **tripped Tufty,** who went tumbling into the grass. Then, she **hurried** to pick the orchid before he could get back up.

"**Hey!**" Tufty hissed. "**Not fair!**"

"Well, you **never said** no tripping," she said.

Tufty only flattened his ears and **glared** at her.

She presented **her colorful collection,** fanned out like a rainbow. "Look at all these flowers," she said, beaming like the square sun. "I guess that means **I win,** huh?"

"**Whatever,**" said Tufty. He threw his clump of dandelions onto the ground. "It was a **stupid** game, anyway."

"I agree," said Eeebs. "**I'm bored.** Maybe we should just head back?"

"**You can't be serious,**" said Meowz.

Tufty stepped forward. "We're not gonna get caught again, okay?"

"I know," said Eeebs. "**But—**"

"Look," said Tufty. "The **only reason** our parents don't want us playing here is because they're **jealous.** They can't stand us kittens having **so much fun.**"

"He's right," said Meowz. "I mean, **have you ever seen any zombies** around here? The truth is they just **cooked up** that story to keep us closer to home. Easier to **make us do chores** that way."

Eeebs **sighed.** Maybe they were right. And anyway, the forest really was **the best place** to play in. There were so many **mysteries** just waiting to be discovered.

"Fine," he said. "How about we go play some **hide-and-seek?**" The other two patted him on the back.

3

"Now you're talking!"

"**Yeah!** That's the Eeebs I know!"

But Eeebs had no idea **how much** this suggestion was going to affect him. He could have seen those dark rain clouds in the distance as **a sign of things to come.** Or the chilly breeze that blew through the meadow just then . . .

He didn't, though. Eeebs was just thinking about **how fun** this day was going to be. A day of playing and exploring. And **misbehaving.**

The three kittens began their new game.

"I think you should go first," Tufty said.

"**Why me?**" Eeebs asked.

"Because this was **your idea,** silly."

Eeebs nodded. He didn't mind. He liked being it way more than he liked hiding. And he knew the **real reason** why Tufty wanted to hide: he liked sitting around, doing nothing. He was a bit out of shape and already out of breath after all of that flower collecting.

As Tufty lumbered off into the bushes, Meowz **smirked** at Eeebs.

"I almost feel sorry for you," she purred. "I know the **ultimate hiding spot.** You're gonna be searching **forever.**"

Eeebs flicked his tail. "I like a challenge."

A real challenge. He wasn't going to be disappointed. . . .

He waited for Meowz to scamper off before **starting to count.**

He reached twenty, called out, and began the hunt. Eeebs bounded through the hills, through the trees. He peeked in every crevice, every clump of tall grass. He raced up and down **all the nearby valleys.**

But he **never found them,** not even Tufty, who was normally easy to find. Were they **hiding together?**

Yes, Eeebs thought. *Meowz must have felt sorry for him and taken him into her **fantastic** hiding spot.*

He searched and searched **to no avail.** Perhaps twenty minutes passed, then thirty. The first **drop of rain** hit Eeebs square on the nose. It started **pouring** soon after.

Grandpa said it was just going to sprinkle, he thought. *This is some sprinkle! At this rate, I'll need a boat!* What happened next sent a shiver down his spine. He walked through some tall ferns . . . and found himself standing at the edge of a **mountainous biome.**

I'm . . .
on the other side of the forest.

He had **never** been this far away from home before. He was so focused on finding them that he hadn't paid attention to his surroundings. **He was lost.**

"Hey!" he called out. "**I give up!** Guys?"

His thin voice was **drowned out** by the torrential rain. Even if his friends were nearby, they wouldn't have been able to hear him. **And they weren't nearby.** Eeebs was sure of that. **They were smart.** They never would have gone this far.

I'm smart too, Eeebs thought. *I'll figure **something** out. I can just follow the edge of the forest. Yeah, as long as I stick to the edge, I'll end up home on the other side. Right?*

He paused. *But what about Tufty and Meowz? Are they **looking for me** right now? Or are they still **waiting** for me? I can't just **leave them.** What should I do?*

The rain grew **heavier.** Eeebs began **shivering.** He decided to go back into the forest and look for them. It was **the right thing** to do. With a **sinking feeling** in his heart, he turned back to the mountains one last time. **A flash of lightning** suddenly lit up the gray expanse, revealing . . . **wolves.**

They were **moving slowly** toward him. His heart sank **even deeper.** If he had seen them, they **must've seen him,** too. Then he heard a **howl.**

His heart was no longer sinking. It was **pounding wildly,** jumping into his throat.

So he started running. He ran fast, very fast. Eeebs had always been good at running, but he'd **never run faster** in his life. Trees blurred past. **Blind panic** set in. He had **no idea** where he was going and didn't care, as long as it was away from those **howls** and **snarls.** Yet **no matter** how fast he went, the sounds stayed behind him.

Wolves could run fast, too.
Very fast.

Eebs dashed **into a thicket.** Cries echoed through the trees. He could hear the wolves snuffling, **sniffing,** searching for his **scent.** That was when he noticed **a purple** glow coming from farther in the thicket. He **turned away** and **crept closer to the light.**

To a **kitten** like him, it looked like **a screen of violet water . . . floating** in the air . . . framed in **black stone.** For a moment, he **forgot about the wolves** completely. He didn't understand what he was looking at. He had **never seen anything like this** before. Well, the humans made things that resembled it called . . . **doors,** but this was something **different.** Whatever it was, it was **very old.** It seemed as if the forest had grown up **around** the strange object.

Was this **the purple light** his mother had warned him of?
It didn't **seem that dangerous.** The light glowed in a **calm** way.
Gentle, even. For some reason, Eeebs felt he should **approach** it. It
was almost as if the doorway was calling to him, **inviting him** to
come closer.

And why shouldn't he? By now, those **mangy mutts** were just
outside the thicket. **Anything** was better than facing them. And the
light was **so warm. Warmer** than any sunlight. Warmer than the
furnace he had slept on that time he snuck into a farmer's house. As
Eeebs drew closer, **the heat washed over him,** removing the rain's
damp chill.

Then, **three wolves burst through the undergrowth.**

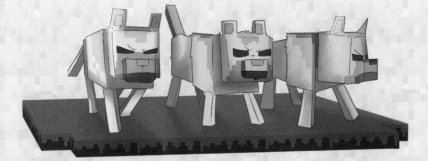

They **stopped** upon noticing the light. Their snarls turned to whimpers, **soft whines.** After some hesitation, they began growling again, their red eyes fixed on Eeebs as they **slunk slowly forward.** He was an **easy dinner,** after all. Those wolves must've seen far worse than a **violet glow. . . .**

Eeebs **backed up,** right next to the light. Heat waves **blurred his vision.** He felt the light behind him, **pulling him closer.** He thought about **his friends.** He hoped they'd make it back **safely.** He was sure they would. Meowz **always knew** how to find her way home.

That was his **last thought** before
diving into the screen of light.

His vision became **blurry,** and suddenly he saw **only** darkness.

Eeebs would **never be a normal cat again.** His days of **climbing trees** and **swatting at butterflies** were over. Stories would spread among the villages, stories of a **strange kitten** with **blue fur** and **violet eyes.**

He hadn't listened to his mom.
He'd ventured into <u>the Nether.</u>

CHAPTER 2

Eeebs **felt nothing** for several seconds. **Nothing** except **his pounding heart.** Bit by bit, the darkness gave way to a **deep red expanse.** It was like an **enormous cave.** Eeebs couldn't see the sky anymore, and **everything was gloomy.** Pillars of **twisted stone** surrounded him. He'd never seen anything like it. Far away, **bright orange streams** flowed down into **a sea** of the same color.

He recognized **this orange stuff.** There was a pool of it in the plains not too far from his home. It was **very hot,** like **liquid fire.** On cold days, the kittens sometimes went near that pool to **warm up.** Of course, his mother had scolded him for hours after finding him there.

*That must be why it's **so warm** here,* Eeebs thought. He turned around, back to **the violet screen.** He had moved **a great distance** by crossing it. Even if he didn't know how, he was certain of this. So that meant he could **head back** at any time. But those **flea scratchers** were probably still waiting for him. If he went back through now, they would **tear him to shreds.**

No, he thought. *I'll stay for now. I'm **safe** here. I only need to **wait** for a while, and . . .*

Just then, **a single wolf emerged from the portal.** It was very close. Eeebs could smell its **rotten breath** and the musky scent of its damp fur. At first he only stared **into the wolf's red eyes,** and it stared back. Neither of them moved. **Total silence.** Then its **confusion** wore off. **Jagged fangs** and a **low growl** shook the kitten into action.

That action, of course, was **bolting across the dark red stones.**

He must be really hungry, Eeebs thought as he jumped across a shallow chasm. *Why **follow** me here? Why couldn't he have just **forgotten about me** and gone after a rabbit?* He zoomed around a column of glowing **yellow rock.** *Rabbits taste better, **don't they?***

Eeebs's path soon came to **an end.** He skidded to a halt on a vast ledge. On each side was a **dizzying** drop. He wasn't afraid of heights, obviously. He was a cat. From countless days of tumbling and tussling in the forest, falling from the **tallest trees,** he could survive **any drop.** He **always** fell feetfirst, but landing on his feet in an **ocean of lava** wouldn't do much good. . . . . And that was all he could see down there.

A fiery orange sea.

The wolf **scrambled** onto the ledge and stopped, knowing it had **cornered its prey.** Eeebs **backed up** against the edge of the abyss. His future seemed **grim. Burned? Or eaten?** If he died now, though, he couldn't **explore** this place. And it **had to be explored!** To a **curious little fuzzball** like him, it was the most **fascinating** place he had ever seen. Forget the forest. Forget the swamp and the ravine. This world would become **their new playground.** Still, he had to deal with this **tail-chaser,** first. . . .

Suddenly, he remembered something that **Tufty** had taught him. When chasing prey, a wolf could get pretty **careless.** The hound surged forward, and Eeebs waited for **the right moment.** Then he dashed to the side with unnatural speed—even for a cat. The wolf's fangs chomped down on **thin air.** That was also the only thing supporting it now: **thin air.** The wolf had leapt **right off the cliff.** It yelped and turned as it fell, **disappearing** over the edge. When Eeebs approached and looked down into the lava far below, there was **nothing.** *Poor wolf,* he thought. **Sadness** washed over him. He had only wanted **to get away. . . .**

Which reminded him: How had he **moved so fast?**

He realized he was **trembling.** His heart was **beating furiously,** and he was suddenly **exhausted.** Eeebs moved away from the edge and sank down onto the ground with **a sigh.** Only an hour ago, he was gathering flowers. **And now . . .**

What rotten luck, he thought. *This is the worst day of my life.* An **icy chill** danced up and down his back. *And it's not over yet. I still have to find my way home.*

That portal would be **easy to spot,** of course, but it **wasn't in sight.** Eeebs had run fast, for a long time, and lost his sense of direction. All of a sudden this new world seemed **much, much larger** and **much more ominous.** Despite the waves of heat, he couldn't help but feel a little **cold.** He curled up into a little ball, pulled his paws in, and wrapped his tail around him.

What should I do? I'm trapped in this gigantic cavern, and I have no idea where to go. But . . . I'm smart. Right? I'll figure something out. Right?

The kitten looked around with big, **fearful eyes,** eyes that shimmered like pools of deep green water.

What will I do now . . . ?
What will I do now?

CHAPTER 3

While Eeebs **trembled in fear,** he started to hear **mysterious noises.** They seemed far away. **In the shadows.**

He could hear piglike **grunts,** horrible **slithering** noises, and something that almost sounded like **crying.** With each new sound, his eyes grew wider and wider. He **shrank back** against the side of a small cliff, his back arched.

Whatever I do, thought Eeebs, *I can't* **panic** *anymore. I'll only get* **more** *lost. I have to think back, retrace my steps.* **That's my only way out.**

Suddenly, the crying seemed **very close.** He slowly turned his head, **afraid** of what he might see. That was when he noticed it: **a kind of small white cloud,** floating in the air. Floating directly toward him.

No, it wasn't a cloud. It had a . . . **face!** Whatever it was, it looked **very sad.** It really was **crying.** A few **light blue tears** were streaming down its cheeks.

"Eeeek!"

The **ghostlike creature shrieked** when it noticed the kitten. Eeebs **sprang back,** tail straight up and fur raised, as if **electrified.** "Leave me alone!" he hissed.

The creature paused and gazed down at itself. "Do I really look **so terrifying?**" The creature sniffled. "I must. Even **this poor little magma cube** can't stand the sight of a monster like me."

It started **crying** again—fountains of sparkling **blue tears,** this time.

"Magma cube?" Eeebs peered cautiously at the bizarre creature. "I'm a kitten."

"A . . . **kitten?**" Its closed eyes shifted with suspicion, ever so slightly. "I don't think I've ever seen a kitten before. You must have come from **a nether fortress,** yes?"

"A forest, actually."

"I don't quite understand." Another sniffle. New tears formed in the corners of its eyes. "Oh, that's why I don't have any friends! I never understand anything about anything!"

Eeebs stepped forward. His curiosity had taken hold. He had so many questions. Besides, it didn't seem like this thing had any intention of eating him.

"Why are you crying? It's a little strange, isn't it? I thought ghosts liked to scare people."

"Ghost?" The white being floated down to the kitten's level. "I'm a ghast. And I'm not strange! Every ghast is sad about something. Some of us cry because there are no flowers here. Others, because it's too hot . . ."

"Well, why are you sad?"

The ghast turned away. "Because I . . . I have no friends. My whole life, that's all I've ever wanted."

The puzzled kitten fixed his eyes on the ghast. Surely, this was the most interesting creature he had ever met. Why couldn't he have found that portal sooner?

"I'll be your friend," Eeebs said.

"What? Oh . . . I get it. A joke, yes?"

"Not at all," Eeebs said. "To be honest, I don't have any friends either. At least, not here . . ."

The ghast turned back to face him. "Really? You mean it?"

"Of course! Why wouldn't I? I'll introduce you to my other friends back home, too."

The ghast spun around in midair. "How can this be? Am I dreaming?"

"I doubt it," said Eeebs, glancing again at this strange new world. "Dreams are never this crazy."

The ghast nodded. He even smiled.

Although neither of them had any idea, this was a special moment. It was the first time in the history of Minecraftia that a ghast had experienced happiness. Their friendship would be documented in books and discussed by scholars and sages for generations to come.

CHAPTER 4

The ghast *(whose name was Clyde)* floated near a chunk of glowing yellow stone. "This is **glowstone**," he said. "It lights up areas that don't have any lava."

"**Lava**," said Eeebs. "That's **the orange stuff**, right?"

"Correct."

For the past **hour or two,** the ghast had explained his world to Eeebs. A guided tour of the **Nether.** The kitten absorbed all of this information, from the **zombie pigmen** to the **blazes** that soared above their heads.

"I wonder if I could bring some glowstone back home with me," said Eeebs. "**It's pretty.** I think my friend—"

"**Ornk-ornk.**" A zombie pigman **bumped into him** with a grunt. Eeebs gasped and **darted** behind the ghast.

"Don't worry," said Clyde. "**He won't hurt you,** remember?"

"Right."

The undead pigman stared at the strange companions before **wandering away.** Clyde went back to the tour. Of course, the kitten's **curiosity** seemed infinite. Every time the ghast answered one of Eeebs's questions, the kitten asked **another.**

Why is there so much lava?
Why are zombie pigmen zombies?
Is there such a thing as a normal pigman?

Only stuff like that. But those endless questions **never annoyed** Clyde. The kitten could have gone on **forever**, and he wouldn't have cared. For the first time in his life, the ghast was helping someone. He was making a difference. **He had a real friend.**

At some point, **a chorus of grunts** and shouts became audible. Far away, across the lava lake, an army of creatures had gathered: zombie pigmen, magma cubes, blazes, wither skeletons—**even an enderman.**

"**Wow!**" said Eeebs. "I've never seen **so many monsters** before! What are they doing?"

"**Causing trouble,**" said the ghast. "You see that tall one? The one with the purple eyes?"

Eeebs nodded. "That's **an enderman,** right? I've seen one before."

"Well, endermen **never** come here," said the ghast. "Except for **him.** His name is **EnderStar.**"

"So why is he here?"

"From what I understand, he was **exiled from his homeworld.** Even the other endermen grew **tired** of his **crazy ideas.**"

The kitten's ears perked up. *Wow. This is way better than playing hide-and-seek, he thought. An army of monsters! An enderman who got kicked out of his own world! What next?*

"Can we get **closer?**"

Clyde paused. "I'm not so sure that would be such **a good idea,** Eeebs."

"**Why not?** Don't you want to **hear** what they're talking about?"

"Well, **all right.** But don't let them see you, okay? They won't care about me, **but if they notice you . . .**"

Eeebs nodded. "How about we **hide on that ledge** over there?"

With that, **the unlikely duo** snuck closer, up a hill that overlooked **the army.** Eeebs peeked out from behind a single block of netherrack.

Clyde **floated** nearby. The monsters below could no doubt see him, but none of them **paid any attention.** He **was** a monster, after all.

Beyond that, everyone was too busy listening to **EnderStar's** speech. All eyes were focused upon that **enderman,** who stood in the middle of the crowd.

"We must take back **what is rightfully ours!**" he shouted, before **pacing back and forth.** He waved a fist in the air. "**We will crush them all!**"

"**Rarg!**" A zombie pigman raised his golden sword. "Crush dem awl!"

The other monsters joined in. The air erupted into an angry chant.

"Crush dem arl!"

"Crush dem awl!"

"Crush dem ull!"

The monsters fell silent when EnderStar waved a hand.

"There's **a portal** not too far from here," he rumbled. "Our **first attack** will commence from there. This is **a practice run,** nothing more. Once you see **how easily their town crumbles,** you will understand the speed with which we can **reclaim our world!**"

A huge **wither skeleton** stepped forward and cut the air with his massive sword. "**Blah, blah, blah!** Talk boring! When me get to **chop things?**"

Another zombie pigman raised his head and screamed. "**Urggrgagrrgr!** Me want smash!"

"**Rargragr!**" One of the blazes trembled with rage. "**Gragragagzzzt!**"

EnderStar **chuckled**—a slow, **smoldering sound** that echoed across the Nether. "**Yes!**" he boomed. "That's the spirit! **Follow me, my brothers!** Let us show them **our might!** Let them bow before us!"

A chorus of shouts shattered the air. The army took off at once, **slithering** and **staggering** across the dark red ground. Their cries faded bit by bit.

"**I don't understand,**" said Eeebs. "What's going on? They're attacking? **Attacking who?**"

Clyde looked away. "Well, **um . . .**"

"**Tell me!**" Eeebs shouted. "I'm **your friend,** aren't I?"

"I . . . I'm afraid they're on their way **to your world.**"

No, Eeebs thought, blood freezing in his veins. *No way. Why would those monsters want to live there? Don't they like this place?* Another **frightening** question spawned in a dark area of his mind.

"Wait," he said. "He mentioned **a portal.** Was he talking about the thing I came through?"

"**Most likely,**" said Clyde.

"So, they're attacking **a city nearby?**"

"**A human city.** Your kind will be safe."

"But what if they **burn** everything?" Eeebs suddenly felt **weak.** His head spun. He **stumbled.** "I have to **get back! I have to warn them!**"

Clyde sighed. "It's **dangerous,** Eeebs. Your mother would want you **to be safe.** You know that."

Eeebs leapt forward, his eyes **filled with anger.** "What if it was **your family,** huh? Would you just sit here? **You want me to . . .**"

As his voice **trailed off,** Eeebs collapsed. He felt so **weak, drained, helpless.** His limbs were like jelly. What was happening to him?

Clyde zoomed down. "Hey! **Eeebs! What's wrong?**"

"I . . . don't know. It's like **I'm . . .**"

"Climb onto me," said the ghast. "I know someone who might be able to help."

"I . . . can't."

"If you want to **help your family and friends,** you will."

Eeebs **took a deep breath.** An image of his mother flashed through his mind. And Tufty. Meowz. All of them. With **the last of his strength,** he pushed himself up and climbed up onto the ghast.

Seconds later,
everything went black.

CHAPTER 5

In her tiny stone hut, Eldra the witch was hard at work.

She hovered over **a brewing stand,** deep in concentration. With one **bottle of water** and one **nether wart,** she created an **Awkward Potion.** Blub, blub, **blub.** The potion burbled to life on the stand. After adding **a dollop of magma cream,** she made a **Potion of Fire Resistance.**

Of course, Eldra **didn't stop there.** It would take only a **pinch of redstone dust** to increase the potion's duration from **three minutes** to **eight.** She did just that, carefully measuring the amount. More bubbles and smoke this time—even **a little flash of fire.** But the extra effort was worth it.

*That will do **nicely,*** she thought. *Now I can go hunting for more **blaze powder** in the fortress nearby. Those silly blazes won't lay a spark on me. Afterward, I could even take **a lava bath.*** The witch giggled to herself. *Just for fun.*

Then she frowned. *But I shouldn't go without at least one **Potion of Regeneration.** Who knows what else I might run into?*

She opened up her ingredient chest and rummaged around. Spider eyes . . . pufferfish . . . blaze powder . . . *no, this won't do at all,* she thought. *Now, where did I put that **ghast tear?***

Sometimes, when a ghast **cries,** one of its tears will **harden** and **crystallize;** this is an **essential** ingredient to make a **Potion of Regeneration.** Unfortunately, this is a **rare** event, so such tears are **highly prized** by witches like Eldra.

And she was **totally out.**

By some **fabulous** twist of fate, however, the answer to her problem arrived right at her iron door.

Clang, clang!

"Who is it?" the witch called out, still searching through her storage container.

"**Me.** Who else?"

Odd, she thought. *Clyde sounds less drooping than usual.*

In her **excitement,** Eldra whirled around, zoomed over to the door, and peered through the window. **Sure enough,** it was him. Was that **the hint of a smile** on his face? He **almost looked . . . happy.** The witch **blinked,** as if she had just seen **a flying cow.**

She hit **the button** to open the door then stepped outside. "You couldn't have come at **a better time,**" she said. "**I need to make a—**"

"Listen, **I really need your help,**" Clyde **gushed.**

Eldra sighed. "Oh, how many times must we go over this, Clyde? Let's stick to our **original deal.** After you've given me **a thousand of your tears,** I will be **your friend.** You only have **eight hundred and eighty-eight** tears to go! See? You're almost there."

What the witch had done was indeed **a little cruel.** The ghast was so **desperate** to make a friend that he'd agreed one year ago to give Eldra **one thousand** of his **crystalized tears.** In return, she would **officially** be his friend. But not really. Not in **her heart.** How could she befriend **a monster like that?**

On the other hand, was it really **so bad** to trick the ghast like this? It was **nicer** than **killing him.** Since their tears were **so valued,** ghasts were close to becoming **an endangered species.** So the witch wasn't **completely** bad. Especially compared to the likes of **EnderStar.**

"It's not about that," said Clyde. "**It's about my friend.**"

Eldra **burst out laughing. "You?"** She giggled again at the thought. **"Have a friend?"**

"As **unbelievable** as it may seem, **yes.** And he's . . . **hurt.** Or **sick.** I don't know."

"Where is he?"

The ghast touched down on the ground. **"Right here."**

The witch approached. She **laughed** again upon seeing the unconscious kitten resting on top of him.

"I won't even ask how you two **met,**" she said. "And what exactly is wrong **with—**"

She froze. Her eyes grew wide all of a sudden. **"It can't be!** This kitten . . . **has the mark!"**

"Mark? What mark?"

Eldra shook her head. "Oh, you foolish ghast! Why didn't you bring him to me sooner? Hurry! Give him to me! There's no time to waste!"

She cradled the limp kitten in her arms then dashed inside her hut.

Clyde floated over to the window and watched Eldra set the kitten down on her blue wool mattress. The witch performed a series of gestures over his motionless body.

That was when he noticed Eeebs's size. He had grown slightly—his claws, too. His fur now had a blue sheen. Was he changing? Why? Was that normal? Did kittens really grow so fast?

"It must have something to do with his illness," the ghast sighed. He felt so helpless. He could only float by the window while the witch performed her magic.

Eeebs will be okay, he thought. *She'll know what to do. I don't know what happened to my friend, but she'll know what to do.*

CHAPTER 6

Eeebs **slowly** opened his eyes.

He was lying on a **soft** surface. He had slept on something like this a while ago: **the farmer's house.** Eeebs liked houses. **Real houses,** anyway. There were so many comfortable things to sleep on in a real house. Stoves. **Beds.** Carpets. Much better than the **hollowed-out log** that served as his home.

No, he was wrong. How could he think **something like that?** His home was a **real house,** too. He remembered the smell of salmon, a smell you'd never find in a house like the farmer's—and **suddenly,** he thought of **his mother,** of **his friends. His home.**

He had to get back. Had to **warn them. Save them.**

Eeebs sprang up. He was in **a stone hut** made of . . . he couldn't remember the word. He tried to recall what Clyde had taught him. Netherrock? Netherstone? No, quartz. **Nether quartz.** That was it. Where was Clyde, anyway?

Just then, he heard **a voice** coming from somewhere outside. **A woman's voice.**

"Don't take this **the wrong way,** but I'm delighted **to see you crying** again," the woman said. "What would I do without your tears? Only **eight hundred and eighty-seven** left, by the way."

"I just hope he'll be **okay.**"

The kitten's ears perked up. *Clyde?*

Eeebs leapt off the bed and through the window. The ghast was just outside, facing **a strange woman** he had never seen before. Both turned to face him.

"**No way!**" said Clyde. "**You're already awake!**"

"Nearly." Eeebs rubbed his face with his paws. "So . . . **what happened?**"

"Something **extraordinary,**" said the witch.

The kitten gave her a confused look. "And who are you?"

"This is **Eldra,**" said Clyde. "She's **a witch.** She's the only one I could think of who could help you. **And she did.**"

"**Honestly,** I didn't do much," she said. "All it took was **a bit of milk,** that's all."

"**I don't understand,**" said Eeebs. "Will someone just tell me what's going on?"

Eldra nodded. "You've been . . . **chosen.**"

"**Chosen?** By who?"

"The Nether."

Clyde floated closer. "The Nether found you, Eeebs. **It called you!** Your arrival here was **no accident.**"

What? That just doesn't make sense, thought the kitten. *Am I dreaming?*

He shook his head. "What would this world want from a kitten like me?"

"Purity," said the witch. "Innocence. **Courage. Love.** You must understand that the Nether isn't an **evil** place. It's filled with **darkness,** but it isn't evil. However, **many of its denizens are.** The Nether needed **a champion,** and when it couldn't find one here, well . . . it looked elsewhere. **It found you.**"

Eeebs **staggered.** It felt like his body was . . . **different.** Well, maybe he was just drowsy—still **a little weak.** He **ignored** these thoughts.

"A **champion** for what?"

But as he asked this, Eeebs realized that this was the one question **he could already answer** himself.

"EnderStar wants to **rule the Overworld,**" said Clyde. "**He's terrible!**"

"And if that happens," Eldra continued, "the **Nether** will be in a **great deal** of trouble. **The End, too.** You see, EnderStar won't stop until **he gains control of all three** worlds."

"I think I get it." Eeebs **paused.** Was he getting **smarter?** He normally wouldn't have been able to grasp this kind of stuff. "The Nether wants to **stop him** before he gets **too powerful,** right?"

The witch smiled. "**Exactly.**"

"But . . . even if I want to help," said Eeebs, "what can I do? **I'm just a kitten.**"

As Eeebs said this, Clyde got **that look** again. It was the *"I don't want my friend to **freak out,** so I'm not going to say **anything**"* look.

Eldra wasn't as considerate. She smirked, looking him up and down.

"Not anymore."

Eeebs followed her gaze.

His black fur had a **vibrant** blue sheen. His claws were a bit **larger,** thick and black. And **sharp.** He was also **bigger** and **stronger**—nearly as big as an **adult ocelot.**

Eeebs held out his paws, examining them, moving each digit. They were almost like **human hands.** "What . . . **happened to me . . . ?**"

"It's not like it's a **bad** change," said Clyde defensively. "I mean, think of it this way: At least you'll **never** have to worry about wolves again."

The witch placed a hand upon his shoulder. **"The Nether changed you. Strengthened** you. And granted you . . . **powers,** you could say. Once you **learn to control them,** the minions of EnderStar will fall before you like **turnips** during a harvest."

The ghast managed a **slight grin.** "I think **'nether kitten'** has a nice ring to it, don't you?"

Eeebs stared down in **horror.** His mind spun and spun. It was just **too much** for him. What would his mother think? His friends?

He would be an **outcast.**
He would become an **exile** . . .
just like **EnderStar.**

Again, Eeebs thought of home. His vision **blurred** as **tears** filled his eyes. He wiped them away with a clawed paw and **nodded** at his two friends. "Thank you, Clyde. Thank you, Eldra."

Then, **he took off.** The Nether's **dull** red terrain streaked past him. "**Wait!**" Clyde called out. "**Eeebs!** There's still a lot **you need to know!**" Eeebs **ignored** his friend's cries. He had wasted **enough time.**

A crazy nightmare, he thought, leaping over a narrow lava stream. *A hallucination brought on by too much stress. Or, maybe this is really happening; maybe the Nether really did turn me into some kind of weird monster.* He **tore across** a ruddy stone plain.

It must have, because he could **sense** the portal's location across all that twisted stone. He pounced up from ledge to ledge and raced through every plateau, until the **glowing violet door** was directly in sight.

He didn't know much about the Nether, what it was capable of, or **what kind of magic** it had placed upon him.

Was it **a curse? A miracle?**

Right now, there was only **one thing** he knew for sure. He was now **a pawn** in a deadly game . . . and he had no choice but to "**play.**"

Armed with this **sole truth,** he cut away his fears and doubts—cut away as if they were just cobwebs in a mineshaft.

Just hold on, he thought, sprinting toward the portal.

Mom . . . Meowz . . . Tufty . . .

I'm coming!

CHAPTER 7

The lava. The inky gloom. The hot netherrack underneath his paws. All of these things the kitten ignored as he ran toward the portal.

He was too busy trying to make sense of it all. **The Nether:** a **dark** world, a **fiery** world, a world that should have **nothing to do with** kittens. But for some reason **this world chose** a kitten to **protect** it. Perhaps a kitten was **a better choice** than a zombie pigman.

Then this world **called** that kitten, **pulling** him from his own world—the bright and tree-filled **Overworld.** Later, the Nether granted him **special abilities** to help him fight the hordes of darkness.

That kitten's name was Eebs.

He's now a **funky-looking** cat.

And Eeebs was trying to **escape the Nether.**

The **intense** heat no longer gave him any trouble. The clouds of smoke, which once **made his eyes water,** were nothing to him. Instead, those eyes were now fixed on the warm light radiating from the portal.

Portal.

His friend Clyde had taught him that word. This portal was a **doorway,** linking two worlds. It looked like a screen of **violet energy,** surrounded by a great ring of black stone.

Eeebs couldn't help but think about Clyde.

*I'm **sorry**,* he thought. *Please **forgive me,** Clyde, for running away without listening to you. I'll **come back.** I have to, because I have to thank you. And **that witch,** too. She removed whatever **illness** I had.*

Eeebs forced himself to **stop thinking** about his new friends.

I'm sure they understand.

Eeebs had to **go through that portal.** He had to leave this world and **return to his own.** Suddenly, it was the **only** real thought in his mind.

No.

There was **another** thought.

Monsters, from this world, were headed to **his own** world. To **attack, to destroy.** To **claim** the Overworld as their own.

Of course, Eeebs had to **warn** his family and friends before that happened.

He slowed down as he neared the portal. Its **enormous** obsidian frame towered before him. All he had to do was step through, as he had before, and **he'd be back.**

His heart **froze.**

He **feared** what he might see upon returning to **the Overworld.** Maybe the monsters had **already** . . .

A frightening image spawned in his mind. . . .

No! There's no way something like that could happen! Those pigmen are too slow!

He pushed such thoughts away, but another **replaced** them.

Enough, he told himself. *I can't waste any more time.*

He leapt through **the purple mist.**

As expected, everything **went black.** He nearly closed his eyes. He was **so afraid** of seeing **something horrible.** But **the darkness** became . . .

Shades of **green, brown. No fire, no ashes.** Nothing was burning. He stepped out of the portal into the thicket where the wolves had almost caught him.

The trees were **still there,** along with the grass and the flowers, and suddenly he realized just how **nice** the forest smelled. He had never thought about it, until now. Actually, **even the swamp** smelled better than the Nether. That place was **horrible** for a kitten's nose.

That was when he caught **another scent.** A familiar scent, like **rotten mushrooms.**

That was the stench of **a zombie pigman. Yuck.**

He sniffed and sniffed, detecting more scents in the air. That ashen smell was from a **blaze,** and that bitter smell no doubt came from one of those **magma cubes.**

They were . . . here.
Somewhere. Somewhere close.
Maybe **just beyond** that large hill.

Relief washed over him. The monsters were stupid and slow— they **hadn't yet** reached his home. It was far from this area, on **the other side of the forest.**

His mind was working **like never** before. The monsters also hadn't reached the village, where the villagers lived. It was **even farther away,** in the plains past the forest.

So since Eeebs was **so fast** now, he could reach his home before the monsters.

Of course, he **did** want to know what those monsters **were up to.** Why were they still here, in the forest?

Shouldn't they have **attacked the village** by now? What could they be **doing?** He hadn't the slightest idea, which meant . . . he **had to find out. He nodded** to himself.

No matter how much the Nether had changed him, it couldn't remove his curiosity.

With his nose as a guide, Eeebs began heading in the direction of the monsters. Slowly, at first, until soon he was bounding over mushrooms and zooming through tall grass.

CHAPTER 8

Eeebs **climbed** up a hill. With every step, **the stench of monsters** grew stronger, and their snarls became **louder.** When Eeebs finally reached the top, he crept low through the grass and peered down the other side.

His pulse quickened. **There they were.**

All of them.

From **blazes** to **wither skeletons.** A snarling, **growling** mass of undead and **fiery beasts.**

And in the middle of them all . . . **EnderStar.** The kitten's fear, however, soon **evaporated.** In fact, he had to keep himself from **laughing.**

He **crept closer** to get a better view.

The monsters, they were . . . **staggering around, stumbling** into one another. At one point, a zombie pigman fell over into the grass.

Then a second pigman **tripped over him,** went flying, and **knocked over** a third.

It was **a ridiculous sight:** an army of **fearsome-looking** mobs, **bumbling around** in a daisy field.

Their distant screams **caught his attention.** Eeebs **perked his ears** up to catch what they were saying.

"It **hurts!**" screamed a zombie pigman. "Mee **eyes!**"

A blaze **hissed** and **sparked.** "Massssshter . . . me no see!"

"**Urgggg!!!**" A wither
skeleton **fell over,** dropping
his stone sword. He **pointed
a bony finger** toward the
sun. "Yellow square thing!
Up there! **Too . . . bright!**"

Another wither skeleton was **chopping at a tree.**

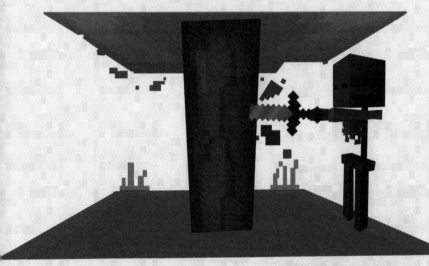

"Mee do good, **mashter?** Look! **Mee chop!**"
A zombie pigman **joined** the skeleton.

"Mee too, **mashter!**"

The wither skeleton's sword seemed to be **stuck** in the tree. "BosSsH, mee sword! The enemy is **so strong!**"

The **huge enderman** let out a long sigh. "That's a tree, **you idiots!!**"

The wither skeleton glanced at **EnderStar** and then back at the tree.

"How can me know, **bossh?** Mee eyes don't work right now!"

The zombie pigman kept chopping at the tree. "**Mee want chop things!** So . . . **mee chop!!**"

A great many zombie pigmen **writhed** on the ground, hands **covering their eyes** as they **screamed.**

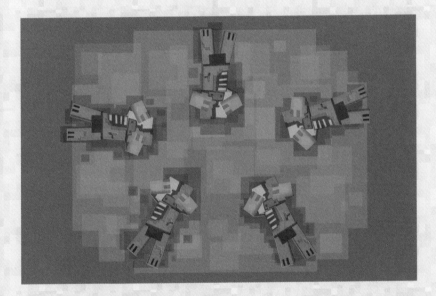

"Urggh! **Mashter!!** Make yellow square go away!"

"It burn! **It burn! Rarrrggg!!**"

"Bossh! You say attack village very easy! **Holp mee!!**"

"**Arggg!!** Villagers use magikk on us!"

"Mashter, mee cannot chop if **mee cannot see!**"

There were lots of shouts like these.

Eeebs only watched in disbelief.

It reminded Eeebs of a scary time, when he'd gone playing in a cave. There had been a big spider in there, and it had chased him for a long time. The spider had run fast, Eeebs remembered. Faster than him. So fast, the spider had caught up to Eeebs by the time he exited the cave. Eeebs had thought he was a goner. All he could hear was that horrible squeak. And then there were those glowing red eyes.

However, when the spider stepped out into the sun, it froze. The spider just sat there, right in front of Eeebs, fangs dripping and eyes gleaming. It couldn't do a thing, because it couldn't see.

That was how Eeebs had learned that spiders were blinded by sunlight. Spiders lived in caves. Their eyes were used to the darkness.

With that in mind, Eeebs now understood why these Nether mobs couldn't see. They shared the same weakness.

The Nether was, in many ways, similar to a cave. When he first arrived there, Eeebs assumed it was just one gigantic cavern.

Even though the Nether had areas filled with lava, it was still pretty dark in most places. So these monsters had lived their whole lives in that gloomy place. Their eyes were used to the darkness. Just like the spiders.

Wow, he thought. *I never could have understood that so easily before. I'm getting smarter, huh? Maybe that's one of the things the Nether did to me? Made me more intelligent?*

Concealed in the tall grass, Eeebs kept **spying.** EnderStar seemed **angrier and angrier.**

The enderman looked up and **shook a fist** at the sky. **"I can't believe this!** All of my planning . . . **ruined** by the **stupid sun!!"**

A zombie pigman **walked up** to the enderman. He was wearing **a golden object** on his head.

"Mee lord? Maybe **we go now** . . . and come back . . . when **no yellow square thing."**

EnderStar **patted** the pigman on the head.

"You're a clever one," he said. "That's why I've made you **a captain."**

"So . . ." The zombie pigman paused. "We go back **now?"**

"Of course." EnderStar's voice **crackled** like lava. **"Gather the troops.** Take them back. This was only meant to be **practice,** anyway. I wanted you all to get some training before we . . . attack **the real village. . . ."**

The pigman **nodded. "Yesh,** mee lord."

Eeebs **squinted,** focusing on the zombie pigman. He seemed **different** from the others. He wasn't **completely stupid,** at least.

51

So that pigman was EnderStar's **assistant?** Also . . . what was that **thing on his head?** Eeebs continued observing the mobs from his hiding spot. His ears were raised up in the direction of the army.

"**Anyway,** today was not **a total waste,**" said EnderStar. "We've learned **something useful.** Next time, we'll come right **after the sun sets.**"

"Of coursh, mee lord. So . . . **you go?** I take pigmen and fire things back now? **We go home?**"

"**Yes,**" said the enderman. "See you back at **the fortress.**"

With that, **EnderStar vanished** into thin air.

POOF!

Eeebs had encountered endermen before. He knew they had **this ability,** so he wasn't too surprised.

EnderStar also said something about a . . . **fortress.**

Fortress.

Clyde had mentioned **that word** before. He thought Eeebs had come from a "**nether fortress.**" So that must be **the monsters'** . . . **home?**

Eeebs needed to **speak with Clyde** about this. After he talked to his friends and family, he had to **return** to the Nether.

Shaking himself from his thoughts, Eeebs looked at the mobs again.

Now **in charge of the other mobs,** the smart pigman turned to his comrades. "**Hey!** All you! **Shut up!** Stop crying! **We go home!**"

Loud grunts and snorts filled the air. "**Home better** anyway," said a wither skeleton. "**Mee no like this place.**"

"**Bzzztrg** . . . t-too **c-c-cold** here," a blaze sputtered. "G-go h-home w-w-warm. **Mee happy!** Argg! **Bzzzt!**"

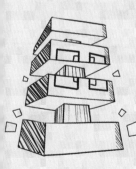

A magma cube **shivered** and hopped in **agreement.**

"But **we no see,**" said a wither skeleton. "We no see! So . . . **how we know where go?**"

"**I can see**," said the smart zombie pigman. He pointed to **the golden object** he wore on his head.

Eeebs had seen humans wearing such things to **protect themselves** in battle. So did that allow the pigman captain to see in the **sunlight?** He really was **smarter** than most zombie pigmen.

"**Follow me**," he said. "I take you home. **All you.** Use ears. **Me sing song. Okay?**"

"Thanks, **Rarg!** Mee so cold!!"

"Okay! **We follow you,** Rarg!"

"**Yes!! Lead the way!** Get mee out of here!"

With that, the captain pigman  *(whose name was apparently Rarg)* began singing.

"Ninety-nine villager noobs in da town! **Ninety-nine villager noobs! Smash one down!** Into **da ground!!** Ninety-eight villager noobs in da town! Ninety-eight villager noobs in da town! Ninety-eight villager noobs . . ."

As he bellowed, the captain **trudged off** in the direction of the portal. The other monsters **followed.** Some began **singing along:**

"Ninety-seven villager noobs in da town! **Ninety-seven villager noobs! Smash one down!** Into—" Rarg **stopped,** turned around.

"**Shut up!** Only I sing! If others sing, how you know **who to follow?**"

"Rarg so **smart!**"

"Okay! **We shut up!**"

Rarg turned back around and began singing and marching again. Eeebs watched them go.

Their little attack failed, he thought. *They must have arrived very early in the morning, just before sunrise. Then the sun came up and blinded them all.*

And they were *stranded*. *Helpless. Helpless* underneath that *overpowering light.*

That means . . . *the Overworld* still has time. Maybe *a lot of time.*

But . . . when they do come back, they'll be more **prepared.**

Maybe, when they return, they'll all have *those golden things* on their heads, like Rarg.

Eeebs didn't realize, of course, **just how well hidden** he was. In fact, as he remained **motionless** in the grass, he had become **nearly invisible.** Without another thought, the kitten **jumped down** the hill.

After he moved, **he became fully visible** again.

CHAPTER 9

Fifteen minutes later . . .

Eeebs was standing outside of **the grove.**

It was where **all of the cats** lived. He could hear playful **meows** in the distance.

Was that . . . **Tufty? Meowz?** He crept through the grass.

He couldn't believe it. He was actually **home?** And . . . he could **see them** now, in the distance.

His friends.
They were playing some kind of game.

"Hey, **not fair!**" hissed Tufty, glaring at Meowz. "You **always** cheat."

"**I didn't cheat,**" she said. "You **never said** no peeking."

"It's always like that," said Tufty. "**You never said this. You never said that.** I miss Eeebs. At least **he played fair. . . .**"

Meowz looked down at the ground, her eyes **full of tears.** "Me too."

Eeebs froze. They were still thinking about him. They were **worried** about him. But what would they think when they saw him? **His fur was blue** now. . . .

He stepped forward anyway.

"I wonder where he is . . . if he's **still alive. . . .**" said Meowz.

"If you ask me," said Tufty, "he went into **that thing.**"

"**Hmm.** Let's go looking for him again."

"Sure, but do you have any idea where **that black thing** is?"

"It's called **a nether portal,**" said Eeebs.

Tufty and Meowz turned to him. The **look** on their faces was **indescribable.**

A piercing sound came from Meowz. "**Eeeeeee . . .**"

Tufty stepped back. "Who . . . **is . . .**" Then, the two seemed to recognize him. "**Eeebs?**"

"Eeebs?" Meowz **cautiously** stepped forward. "**Is that . . . really you?**"

Eeebs nodded.

"What . . . **happened** to you?"

"I'm the one who should ask," Eeebs said.

"You went **in**," said Tufty. "**Didn't you?** You actually . . . **went into** that place?"

The kittens knew **stories** of the Nether, although they didn't call it by that name. Stories about **the black door.** The glowing **purple light.** Old stories. Legends telling how the **bravest** and **strongest** cats once went through that door. And **never came back.**

Eeebs, however, had come back.

Maybe he had been **lucky** to meet Clyde, who taught him **all about** that world. Or maybe it wasn't luck. Eeebs had thought nothing of talking to Clyde. But an older, wiser cat probably wouldn't have **tried** talking to a ghast. An older, wiser cat would have **simply run.**

Just as Eeebs had **ignored** the legends and the warnings from his mother, he'd also ignored his **common sense**—which generally encouraged **running away** from giant white flying things that **cried** and **shot balls of fire** from their mouths.

Who knew there could be a ghast who was actually **kind?** That was why Eeebs had survived.

As Tufty and Meowz stood before him, **in awe,** Eeebs told them about all his adventures. What happened to him. How he **changed.** How the Nether had **chosen** him.

"**Chose you for what?**" asked Tufty.

"To help **fight** against that army," said Eeebs. "I guess."

Then, Eeebs told them about how an enderman was **planning to take over their own world.**

"So let me get this straight," said Meowz. "That place, the Nether, chose you? To be some kind of **warrior?** And you have like . . . **special powers** and stuff?"

Eeebs nodded again. "Basically, **yeah.**"

"**Wow,**" said Tufty. "That's **too cool,** huh? **Special powers?** Fighting **bad guys?** And honestly, Eeebs, you don't even look that **scary!** Where do I sign up? **I wanna help you!**"

"By the way, what kind of powers do you have, anyway?" asked Meowz.

"Well, **I don't know,**" said Eeebs. "I mean, Clyde and his friend were about to tell me more about **the change,** but . . . I ran off before they could. I just wanted to **find you guys.**"

"**Awww.**" Meowz's eyes grew even more tearful. "**Thanks.**"

"A **good friend,**" said Tufty. "Us too. We looked for you everywhere, you know? We haven't really slept since you disappeared. Anyway . . . I'm just **glad** you're back."

Eeebs sighed. "Me too, but . . . at some point, I'll have to go . . . back there."

All three of them looked down at the ground. Then, **a cry broke the silence.**

"Eeebs?"

It was his mother.

CHAPTER 10

Eeebs's mother **carefully** approached the three kittens. She looked like Eeebs *(the old Eeebs, anyway)*, only bigger.

Eeebs only **swallowed,** his eyes **wide.**

"**Oh boy,**" whispered Tufty. "Things are gonna **get crazy.**"

Meowz joined him in cowering.

"This isn't good," she murmured. "She scolded Eeebs **for days** just for going too close to the **fire lake,** over in the plains. How do you think she'll react to **this?**"

His mother was now quite close, and as she noticed her son, she couldn't hide her **astonishment. "Eeebs Cottonpaw Thistlewhiskers,** what on Earth happened to you?!"

"Mom, **I can explain,**" said Eeebs, his ears **lowered,** tail **between his legs.** "You see, **there's this—**"

"**Enough!**" she hissed. "You'll explain this to **your father!**"

She picked him up by **the scruff of his neck** and hauled him off to their **cat burrow.**

Tufty and Meowz exchanged **worried glances.**

CHAPTER 11

For half an hour, Eeebs **stared at the floor** as his mother **scolded** him. Of course, he tried telling her about what had happened. But she **wasn't hearing any of it.**

"I told you not to go near **that door!**" she said. "Cats have no business in there!"

"**I'm okay,** Mom. **Really.** Maybe what happened to me is a **good** thing."

"**Good?**" She turned away. "How can it be good? You look so **different** now. Your fur, it's . . . it's . . . **it's blue!**"

Eeebs rubbed up against his mom.

"**Hey.** I'm sorry for going in there, but . . . monsters really **are** going to **attack our world.**"

"Well, what can we do about it?" she said. "Let the humans deal with it. And those . . . . villagers."

"I don't think it's that simple," Eeebs said. "I mean, the mob army is **huge.** I've seen it with **my own eyes.**"

This made his mother even **more worried.** "And what exactly are **you** supposed to do?"

Eeebs sighed. "**I don't know,** Mom. But there must be **a reason.** That's what Clyde said. **He's a ghast.** Oh, and his friend, Eldra. **She's a witch.** She said—"

62

"Ghast?!" his mother yelled. "**Witch?!** Young man, you won't go near those things again! **Do you understand?**"

"But they're **my friends.**"

"**Friends?!** No, you won't be making friends with **monsters!**"

"Not all monsters are **bad**, Mom. . . . Clyde is really, **really nice.**"

His mother was **really upset** now. "Just wait until your father hears about this! You're lucky he's **out hunting** right now!"

"Mom, please just **calm down. . . .**"

It went on like this for some time. Like most mothers, she was **a bit overprotective.**

His father eventually **came back,** carrying some salmon. He was a good hunter.

When his father noticed Eeebs, he dropped the salmon on to the grass floor of their house.

"**Son?** What . . . **happened?**"

And so, Eeebs explained **all over again.** Thankfully, his father **wasn't as upset.** He almost seemed **proud** of Eeebs.

"The Nether **chose** you?" he said. "I don't like it, but . . . this must be **important.**"

"**What are you saying?**" said his mother.

His father flicked his tail, **thinking** for a moment. "I just think we should **try** to learn more about this."

"I can't believe you're saying this!" His mom circled back and forth.

"Honey, we can't do anything about it. What happened . . . happened."

His mother sighed. Then, there were several cries outside.

"Monster! Run!!"

Eeebs glanced at his mom and dad then dashed outside.

CHAPTER 12

A crowd of cats and kittens **scattered** in **terror.**

A witch walked out from behind a massive oak tree.

"**Eeebs!**" she shouted. "Eeebs! **Are you there?** Oh, there are so many kittens, but none of them are the one I'm looking for! At least, I don't think any of you are Eeebs. . . . **Blue fur? Purple eyes?** No, no, **no!** Where is he?!"

The few remaining kittens **squealed** and ran off to their parents. But one kitten remained.

Eeebs **slowly** walked toward the witch.

The other felines **crouched** in their hiding places, watching Eeebs approach what appeared to be **a hideous monster.** *(Actually, to them, Eeebs appeared like a monster as well.)*

"**Eldra!**" Eeebs said. "How did you get here?!"

"Same as you. I simply **went through the portal,**" Eldra said. "I'm from **the Overworld** too, you know!"

Suddenly, Eeebs's mother and father ran up to him. "**Get away** from that thing, Son! **It's dangerous!**"

"**Dangerous?**" The witch giggled. "Yes, I suppose I am dangerous! But only when I have **potions,** and I'm all out."

"**Enough!**" said Eeebs's father. "Leave our son **alone!** He will not associate with the likes of **you!**"

The witch **cackled**—an eerie, high-pitched sound. This caused some other kittens in the distance to begin **crying.** After the witch stopped laughing, Eeebs **sighed.**

"Mom, Dad, **meet Eldra.** Eldra's a witch. But she's **really, really nice.** She helped me when I got sick. I wouldn't be **alive** if it weren't for her. So you should **thank her.**"

His parents peered at Eldra.

"You don't have to praise me," said Eldra.

A bat flew past her. She **grabbed** it. "**Ooooo! How lucky! I** need bat wings!" The witch stuffed the **squeaking** creature into her belt pouch.

His parents backed away, **making low growling sounds,** pulling Eeebs along with them.

Eldra continued. "Actually, your son is **special.** I'm certain he would have survived, even **without my help!**"

"**No way,**" said Eeebs. "I was so sick. My stomach was roiling, and I passed out, and—"

"**Stop it, Eeebs!** Just stop!" His mother was beginning to weep again. Then she wiped her face with a paw and turned to Eldra. "Is it true? You . . . **helped our son?**"

Eldra nodded.

"Who wouldn't help a lost kitten? Besides, he's got **the mark!**"

"**Mark?** What do you mean?" asked Eeebs's father.

"I can tell you what I know," said Eldra. "But first . . . let the rest of your kind know: I wish you no harm. In fact, if you want to **survive** . . . you'd best listen to me."

And so Eeebs's parents finally **calmed down.**

The rest of the felines eventually crept back—but **cautiously, slowly, very slowly.**

At last Eldra began to tell everyone the history of **Minecraftia. . . .** How an **innocent** kitten came to befriend a nice ghast named Clyde . . . And how an **evil** enderman, exiled from the End, **rose to power** in the Nether . . .

CHAPTER 13

After perhaps an hour of talking, Eeebs said his goodbyes to everyone he knew. His mother and father were in tears.

"In case we get attacked," said his father, "we'll dig **a small cave** nearby. That way we'll have a place to run and hide."

Eeebs nodded.

"**Good idea.** And don't cry, huh? I'll be back soon! **I promise!**"

Then Eeebs turned to his **two best friends.** Strangely, Tufty and Meowz didn't seem upset. In fact, they seemed a bit **happy.**

Am I just imagining things? Eeebs thought. *How can they not be sad? Even I want to cry right now!*

"I wish you didn't have to go, Eeebs," said Meowz. "**I'll miss you.**"

"**Same here,**" said Tufty. "I'm **so sad. So sad.** But hey, you've gotta do what you've gotta do."

Eldra the witch smiled at Eeebs's mother and **patted** her head.

"Don't worry," Eldra said. "Your son just needs **some training.** I'll do my best. He'll be back soon. I **promise.**"

With that, Eldra and Eeebs took off, back to **the portal.**

CHAPTER 14

Five minutes later, Eeebs already missed his parents. And his friends. He hadn't even been home for more than two hours.

But then, his heart **grew lighter** at the thought of seeing Clyde again. Upon entering the Nether, Eldra led Eeebs back to her **stone hut.**

"I've been meaning to ask," said Eeebs. "As you said, **you come from the Overworld.** So why do you have a house in the Nether?"

The witch **sighed.** "Well first, it's called **a hut.**"

The kitten looked up at her, waiting for her answer. The witch continued.

"Brewing," she said. "**Nether wart. Blaze powder.** The Nether has a lot of things I need. So, I decided to build **a second hut** here."

She opened the door. "Now, **let's begin.**"

Eeebs followed Eldra inside. She walked over to the cauldron. **The purple liquid** bubbling within it smelled **strange** yet **delicious** at the same time.

"**Mushroom-bat stew,**" she said. "Care for some?" Eeebs's stomach **grumbled** as the witch said this.

How sad, Eeebs thought. *I didn't even eat anything while I was at home. I should have grabbed some salmon . . . or a pufferfish. I'm not picky!*

"**Sure,**" he said at last.

The witch set a steaming bowl of stew on to the floor. The kitten **lapped it up** hungrily. Actually, it **wasn't that bad.**

"Now," said Eldra. "Before we start, let me tell you: You're not the only **strange creature** walking around Minecraftia."

The kitten's ears **perked up.**

"You mean there are **others like me?**"

Eldra shrugged. "In a way."

"Like what?"

"Well, during **a full moon,** one out of a hundred spiders that spawn are granted special powers **similar** to yours. **The Dark Blessing,** it's called. Some can **heal** their wounds **quickly.** Others are **impossible to see** or possess **incredible** strength. And then there are creepers, who become **much stronger** when struck by **lightning.** Pigs struck by lightning turn into **zombie pigmen.** And where do you think I came from? I used to be **a villager,** you know . . . until I went out in **that thunderstorm. . . .**"

Eeebs **scratched** his chin. "Is all that related to the **Nether,** like me?"

"Not exactly. Still, there are many unusual creatures wandering around. **So don't feel alone.**"

"Thank you."

Eldra smiled. "As for **your powers . . .**"

"Yes," said Eeebs. "You've mentioned that before. What are they?"

"Well, first, you're probably already aware that you can **think** more clearly."

Eeebs nodded. "I've been able to **figure stuff out** on my own way easier than before."

"And your senses are **sharper,** correct?"

The kitten nodded again. "I can **sense nether portals** and even see in the dark better than before."

"Of course." The witch gazed into his **purple eyes.** "From what I've read, the spider's **Dark Blessing** also affects you, in limited form. If you **stand still,** you'll be nearly **invisible.** I'm not sure what you have to do to **heal** faster, though. Beyond that, you'll find that you have **the powers of every mob** native to the Nether."

"What does that mean?" asked Eeebs.

"For one, you're all but **immune to fire.** Including lava."

Lava, Eeebs thought. *That's that fiery orange stuff!*

"You mean I **won't be hurt** by it?!"

"Not at all," said the witch. "You can **swim around in it** all day if you want, and it won't even singe your whiskers."

At this point, the kitten's **curiosity** was overflowing. He didn't have to fear the Nether anymore! He could **explore** as much as he wanted!

Wait, he thought, *how can I **think** about exploring at a time like this?!*

"What else?" he asked.

"**Hmm.** You can **spit fireballs** the same way a ghast can, and I'm guessing you have a **Wither** effect, like all wither skeletons. And a zombie pigman's **strength.** Perhaps you can even **fly** like a blaze? But you'll have to learn how to do all of that **from the mobs**

72

themselves. Of course, I believe you have **even more** special powers, but I must research more. I haven't had much time, since I had to go looking for you."

"This is **so great!**" said Eeebs.

"Indeed. When you come to understand your strengths, you'll basically be **a boss** monster, like the **ender dragon** or the **wither**. Cool, huh?"

"What are those?" Eeebs asked.

"Oh, **never mind.**"

The kitten sighed. "Whatever. I **can't wait** until Clyde teaches me how to shoot fireballs. Where is he, anyway?"

The witch looked down at the floor. "**Um . . .**"

"What?" The kitten crept forward. "What is it? **Where is he?**"

"Well, it really hurts to say this, **but . . .**" The witch turned around. "Shortly after you left, Clyde . . . joined **EnderStar's army.**"

Eeebs stepped back, slowly. The words repeated in his head, **over and over.**

Clyde. Joined EnderStar's army.

Clyde.

A happy ghast.

*A nice guy. **Helpful.** Cries at the slightest hint of bad news.*

*And he joined . . . **those monsters?!***

"I . . . I don't get it. . . . **Why?**"

"I don't know," said Eldra. "He tried **following you,** but ghasts can't fly very fast, you know. He couldn't even find the portal. I've never seen a ghast **shed so many tears.** He kept asking me where the portal was, how to find you. I'm not a tour guide! Then **he just floated away.**"

A single tear ran down the kitten's cheek. "I . . . **can't** . . . believe this. . . ."

"**Be strong,**" said Eldra. "There must be a good reason why he did something like that. **Believe in** your friend."

Eeebs looked up at Eldra again. "I have to go **find him!**"

"**Of course you do.** You should stay here first, though, and **train** with me . . . but you're not going to do that, are you?"

"**Not a chance,**" said Eeebs, shaking his head. "**I owe him.**"

"Then you'll want to head to **the nether fortress.** It's **that way.**" She pointed out the window. "You can't miss it."

Eeebs glanced out the window, then back at Eldra. The witch gave him a **blank look.**

"**What?** Are you expecting me to ask you to stay here? I know you by now, Eeebs. You'll go. You'll do anything to save your friend. There's simply nothing I can do."

"You're right, just . . ."

"**What?**"

"Do you have **any advice** for me? It's not like I've ever been to a nether fortress."

Eldra took out **a book** from her item chest.

"The best piece of advice I can give you is to **write in this** every day. It's called **a diary.** Within its pages, you can record your experiences and any important information."

"But I don't even know how to write! Or spell. Or read. **I'm a kitten.**"

"**Wrong,**" Eldra said. "That's another one of your abilities. I forgot to mention that."

"But even if I know how to write, I can't **hold a quill!**"

Eldra handed the kitten a quill. "Haven't you noticed your paws are a little **different?**"

Eeebs glanced down at his paws, held each one in front of him, and then grabbed the quill.

"**Unbelievable.**"

"What's so hard to believe?" asked Eldra. "This is **Minecraftia.**"

"**Right.** So . . . book, quill, anything else?"

"You're **smart.** You'll figure out the rest. And do bring Clyde back. He owes me more tears."

"**Count on it.**"

Once again, Eeebs took off **without much hesitation.** He had an inventory, a diary, a quill, and **a whole lot of courage.**

But how am I going to sneak into a nether fortress? he thought. What's Clyde doing, anyway?

Why did he join that **crazy army?** Was he **angry** because I took off? **What happened?**

CHAPTER 15

Eldra watched the kitten zoom off into the Nether.

"He's sure got **spirit**," she said to herself. "I think he'll be just fine."

She went back into her hut, glanced at the bubbling cauldron, at the brewing stand, and finally . . . her mat on the floor. It was just **carpet**, but it was the best she could do. **Beds exploded** in the Nether, for whatever reason.

She **suddenly** felt **exhausted.** She yawned, headed over to her mat, and . . . heard **a mewing** sound coming from just outside her hut.

What's that noise? she thought. *It almost sounds like a kitten! But . . . what's Eeebs doing back so soon?*

The witch, **thoroughly confused,** went outside and glanced around. Lying nearby, on the reddish netherrack, was **not just one** kitten, **but two.**

They looked **sickly,** barely conscious, as Eeebs had been after he'd **first entered** the Nether.

However, they didn't look like Eeebs at all. One had **tan fur with orange stripes.** The other, **light gray and brown** with **bright blue eyes.**

Both kittens soon stopped moving, having lost consciousness.

Eldra **carefully** approached them. She realized she wouldn't be getting sleep anytime soon. She needed **two buckets of milk** to cure their illness, and she was **fresh out.**

I wonder, she thought. *Can I bring a cow into the Nether?*

She bent down and picked up the two kittens, one in each arm, then took them into her hut and laid them on her mat.

Of course, she wasn't **surprised** when she examined them.

Like Eeebs,
both kittens had the mark.

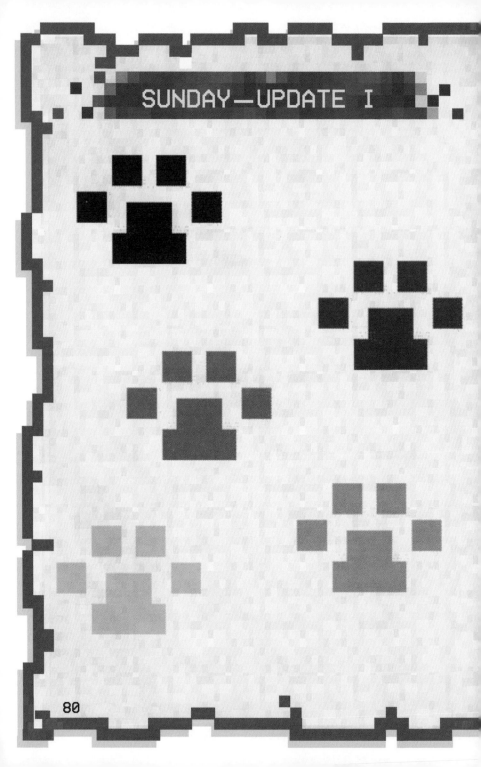

Meow?

Okay. There we go. I **finally** figured it out.
Apparently, I needed to use
a chicken feather, not my paws.

So, where do I begin? **My name is Eeebs.** I'm a kitten. Well, sort of. I'm a little **different,** nowadays.

What happened? I still don't know completely. I was just trying to get away from those **wolves.** Then I found that **nether portal.** . . .

After I stepped through, **I began changing.** I found that I could run **faster,** jump **higher.** Even turn slightly **invisible.** This witch I met said I could even gain **the abilities of monsters.**

Plus, I'm **way smarter** than I used to be. After all, kittens don't typically have diaries.

The witch said there's a reason why all of this happened. I've been **"chosen"** to help save the world. There's this **huge army** of monsters, and they want to take over **all three** dimensions.

Of course, I'm supposed to **help stop** them. Me. **A kitten.** I find that **hard to believe.**

The only thing I've ever been good at is **chasing bats around.** I'm pretty sure there's **a lot more** to saving the world than that.

Anyway, for now I'm putting all that aside. You see, during my time in the Nether, I also made **a friend: Clyde.**

He's a ghast. He taught me a lot of things about his world. But then, the witch said he took off to **join that army.**

My best buddy, siding with the **enemy?** Clyde would never do that! And if he did, it must have been for a very good reason. Maybe he's **spying** on them. Or maybe they **forced him.**

In the end, it doesn't matter **why** he left. I have to go **find** him.

The witch said that Clyde took off to this place called **a nether forest.** Was she **joking** around with me? I don't think the Nether even **has** forests.

I've been searching for **hours**
and haven't found **a single tree.**

SUNDAY—UPDATE III

I **searched around the Nether** some more.

At first, all I found were **mushrooms, glowstone,** and a lot of zombie pigmen.

Then I saw **a weird creature.** He was stranded in the middle of a lava lake, **balancing** on a single block of netherrack.

The Nether is full of **strange stuff,** but I've never seen anything like it before. I just had to see what he was doing there.

But as I got closer, I noticed that this creature **looked unfriendly.**
Dangerous, even. He was made of bones and was carrying **one of those sharp things** the pigmen always have on them.

Just as I turned away, he shouted:

"Hey! Don't **leave,** huh?! I really need some **help** over here!"

My **curiosity** got the best of me. I turned back and approached the lava.

"How can I **help?**" I called out, stepping to the lake's edge. "I **can't swim in lava.**"

"**Sure you can,**" he said. "You won't **burn up!** Just hop in, float over here, and **give me a ride!** Wait . . . you **are** a magma cube, aren't you?"

"Actually, **I'm not.**"

The creature leaned forward slightly, as if taking a better look. "**Oh, sorry!** My vision's not the best these days. Well, if you're not a magma cube, what **are** you, then?"

His question totally **threw me off guard.**

How could someone **not** know **a kitten** when they see one? Even one such as myself . . .

"What do you mean, **what am I?!**" I hissed. "**What are you?!**"

The bony figure whirled around, apparently just as **shocked.**
"**What?** Haven't you ever seen **a wither skeleton** before?!"

"I have," I said. "But only a few times, and I never knew what you guys were called. I'm from the **Overworld. Long story.**"

"Right. Some other time." The **so-called** skeleton paused. "**Got a name?**"

"Eeebs. You?"

"Batwing." He glanced around. "Well, Eeebs from the Overworld, how about we help each other out?"

"Assuming I even could get you out of there," I said, "what would you do for me?"

The skeleton laughed. "Simple. You need a guide. You're clearly lost. I mean, if you knew anything about this place, you wouldn't be going that way. No, anywhere but that way."

I glanced in the direction I'd been heading earlier.

All I could see were netherrack hills, nether quartz veins, and lavafalls.

"It doesn't look so bad," I said, pretending not to care. But again, my curiosity soon took hold. "What's over there, anyway?"

"More of my kind," Batwing said, "plus a whole lot of blazes. And none of them are as nice as me. Believe me, fuzz block, the last place you want to be going to is a nether fortress."

My ears perked up. Nether fortress . . . ?

So that explained why I never found any trees. I thought the witch had said nether forest, but I must have misheard.

This whole language thing is still new to me. I could speak with other cats before, yes, but my conversations with other creatures were . . . very limited. The only non-cat word I knew before this change was "grr," which is wolf for "I'm going to eat you now."

After realizing what the skeleton had said, I was **so excited** that I stepped to the very edge of the lake and **nearly slipped off.**

"**A nether fortress?!** That's exactly where I need to go! **My friend went there!** I need to **save** him!"

"You've got to be **kidding** me. . . ." The wither skeleton lowered his head. "And here I thought it was **my lucky day.** . . ."

"The deal's still on, right?"

The skeleton shook his head. "**No. No deal. No way** am I going there."

"Fine." I turned around. "Then I'll just have to go there myself. **See you around!**"

"**N-no, w-wait!**" the skeleton called out. "Okay! **You win!** Just get me off this rock, and I'll take you **anywhere you want** to go."

I nodded. "What do I do?"

"**That's easy.** Since you can't swim, you're going to be **building** a bridge."

Bridge? Another word I didn't know. Clyde had taught me a lot of words, but he'd **never mentioned** anything about bridges.

"A what?"

"**Seriously?** They don't have bridges in the Overworld, either?"

"Maybe they do, but I've never heard of them. Also, what's 'building'?"

Batwing **grumbled** to himself. "**Never mind.** I'll walk you through it. You don't happen to have any tools, do you?"

My confusion only grew. "Tools?"

More grumbling from **my new friend**. He glanced downward, particularly at my paws. Then he **chuckled**.

"Y'know, actually, I think **we can make this work.**"

"Come on! **Punch!**"

A skeleton named **Batwing,** surrounded by lava, shouted these words at me. It's been a weird couple of days.

Still near the shore, I stared down at **the reddish netherrack** beneath my paws. "So, **I just hit it?** Like this?"

"**Exactly! But harder!**"

I threw a real punch this time.

Cracks formed where my paw struck the ground. Only, they vanished as quickly as they had appeared.

"**Don't stop!**" Batwing called out. "Just **keep punching!**"

"Seems a little **weird.**"

"**It's not!** It's what you have to do when you don't have any tools!"

"Right." More punching.

My paws hammered away at a block of netherrack.

I didn't let up this time—just kept punching away. The cracks grew **larger and larger,** until finally the block **came loose.** I pulled it out without too much effort.

It **wasn't as heavy** as I'd expected.

Batwing seemed **pleased.** "**That's it!** Now, just place it over by the edge there!"

I did as he instructed. Since I was holding the block with my front paws, I had to stand upward on my hind legs.

I was walking. Just like a zombie pigman. Only **not as fast.** Hobbling over, I shoved the block against the edge of the shore. Strangely, **as if by magic,** the block snapped into place.

I'd **never known** that it was possible to change the environment like this. Truly, I understood nothing about **the rules of this world.** *(Even if I am smarter than the average kitten, I still have a lot to learn.)*

"**Great work** so far!" Batwing said. "Now, do it **five more times!**"

I glanced at the lava between us. Suddenly, **it all made sense.**

If I placed enough blocks, a row of netherrack would be formed across the lava, a so-called **"bridge."** *(Gosh, these monsters and their fancy words!)*

Punch, **punch.**

I moved a **second** block. **A third.**

Finally, after I placed the **sixth,** Batwing jumped **so high** it was almost as if he could have cleared the lava without a bridge at all.

Then he **zoomed** to safety, stopped, spun around, and **jumped again.** "Oh, man! I can't believe this! You don't know how **thankful** I am, kitten! I was **trapped** there for **weeks!**"

"Now that you mention it," I said, walking up to him, "exactly **how** did you wind up there?"

Batwing looked away. "**Those animals! They** put me there! After I told them we shouldn't be attacking the Overworld!"

"Who's **'they'?**"

Then it hit me. "You mean you were part of **that army?**"

"**Yes. Was.** I couldn't go along with everything they were doing. That enderman is **crazy.**"

I knew he must have been talking about **EnderStar**—an enderman **so bad** his own kind actually **kicked him out of the End.**

"**By the way,**" Batwing went on, "you should know that **not everyone** in the Nether is bad. Like my friends. I'd like to **introduce you** to them."

"**That's fine,**" I said. "But first . . ."

"Yeah, **yeah, I know.** We'll find your friend. But let's get **one thing** straight first."

"What's that?"

"**I'll do all the talking.**"

We finally reached **the fortress.**

I'd never seen anything **so big**—just **block after block** of nether brick. Another so-called **"bridge"** spanned a wide chasm filled with more orange fire water. A wither skeleton was **standing guard** there.

"That's **Wishbone,**" Batwing whispered. "Not too smart, but an **all right** kind of guy. Just follow me and don't say anything. Actually, wait. Make **a hissing sound.** Can you do that?"

I hissed. "**Like this?**"

"Kind of. But more like **smoldering magma** or something."

"**Magma?**"

Batwing **facepalmed.** "Dude. You **have** seen a **magma cube** before, right?"

"Maybe? **I don't know?**"

"**Whatever.** After we go up to him, just start **hissing.**"

"Okay."

Batwing walked up to the wither skeleton, and I followed.

"I never thought you'd **make it off** that block," Wishbone said, "with your **fear of swimming** and all. Anyway, the boss said you aren't exactly **welcome** here anymore."

"That's fine." Batwing pointed at me. "I just wanted to show the boss this, and then I'll be on my way."

92

"Huh? What's that?"

"A **very rare** type of magma cube," Batwing said. "Might be useful for the army."

Wishbone approached me. "Doesn't look like any magma cube **I've** ever seen. Aren't they supposed to look like, **um,** you know, magma?"

Batwing **shook his head.** "As I said, this is an **extremely rare** type. And **very powerful,** I might add." He glanced at me. "Plus, it **hisses,** just like any magma cube."

Oh. **Right.**

I hissed **as loud** as I could.

"What kind of sound is **that?!**" Wishbone said. "Listen, it doesn't sound like a magma cube at all, and why is it **blue?**"

Batwing sighed. "You're **making fun** of a poor little magma cube because he's **blue,** are you? You know the boss doesn't like such **discrimination!**"

"**N-no,**" Wishbone said. "I—"

Batwing shook his fist, seemingly **angry.** "So **he's blue!** So what?! Do you know how many monsters have **made fun of him** for this?"

"I was just **joking!**"

"**Clearly!** A joke at **his** expense!"

"**I'm sorry!** Please **come in!** Don't tell anyone I said that!"

"Fine. And don't tell **anyone** we're here," Batwing said. "I want EnderStar to be **surprised** when he sees his new **gift.**"

"Y-yeah, okay, okay." Wishbone looked at me. "Sorry, man. Blue magma cubes are **totally cool,** all right? Even blue magma cubes with **legs!**"

"Hissss?! Hisss! Hiss-**hiss**-hiss!!"

"I said I'm sorry!" He stepped backward and made a wide gesture. "Come on in."

With that, we walked past him and stepped inside the fortress.

"You're probably wondering why that guy was **so afraid,**" Batwing said once we were out of earshot. "From what I've heard, EnderStar was **picked on** as a kid because his eyes glowed **too brightly.**"

"I certainly know how it feels," I said. "So, any monster under his command who makes fun of another's **appearance** is **punished?**"

"**Yeah.** Something like that."

As we wandered farther inside, I began to realize just how **huge** the nether fortress was: Endless halls stretched for **hundreds** of blocks.

There were **so many monsters** here, too. I'd seen most of them before. Batwing told me the **angry fire things,** floating in the air, were called blazes. More wither skeletons **marched in groups,** along with zombie pigmen. I even saw a few ghasts **floating around** in the larger chambers. **Sadly,** none of them were Clyde.

Another wither skeleton soon **stopped** and questioned me:

"**Hey! You there!** What are you, exactly? You're the **strangest-looking monster** I've ever seen!"

"I am **Lord Sizzleblock**," I said, "**Royal** Magma Cube from the Overworld. EnderStar has asked me to pay him a visit. **And you are?**"

"Yes, let us know **your name**," Batwing said, "so that **the noble Lord Sizzleblock** can inform the **great** and **powerful** EnderStar of such **discrimination** and—"

The skeleton fell to his knees and **bowed** so deeply he all but kissed the nether brick floor. "Forgive me at once, **Your Majesty!** I simply didn't know that your kind came in such **lovely shades** of blue! How many times do you want me **to bow?**"

"**Fifty** should be enough," I said.

"Of course, **my lord!**"

Every time a monster **questioned us,** it went pretty much like that.

Once, a zombie pigman grunted at us. "**Urg!** Who you? Why you here?" He looked closer. "**Urguu?!** What you are?!"

Batwing pointed his sharp stick at the **zombified** pigman. "How **dare** you address the **grand** and **majestic King Flamepixel** with such insolence! He visits upon EnderStar's request, who shall be **notified** of your—"

The zombie pigman **didn't apologize.**

Instead, he **ran off** the nearby edge of the fortress—**without jumping,** just kind of **tipping** over—and fell into the lava far below. The way he dropped off instead of jumping . . . it was like he wanted to reach the lava **as fast** as zombie pigman-ly possible, to the millisecond.

(In case you were wondering, we were in an open section of the fortress at this time.)

"**Wow**," I said. "Um . . . that was a **pretty extreme** reaction, no? They must **really** fear EnderStar."

Seconds later, a blaze appeared. "**Gzzzzt?!** Www-w-what?! Bgzzzt!! **A-a-are?!** Gzrrg!! Y-y-ou . . . ?!"

I stepped forward, **about to say something.** I didn't need to, though. Not this time. The blaze was **very confused** by the sight of me. So bewildered, in fact, that it began **trembling** in the air, made a weird **sputtering** noise, and flew off while spinning around and **gurgling**—its direction and angle changing **randomly** as it did.

96

I watched the blaze **disappear** into the gloom overhead. "Do I really look **that weird?**" The sputtering sound eventually faded completely.

Then I heard a voice in the distance.

"**Eeebs?!**"

There he was, gliding through the air.

"**Clyde!** What are you doing here?! I've **been looking everywhere** for you!"

"Oh, Eeebs. **I'm so sorry.** I . . ."

"Did you really **join their army?**"

"**Yes,**" he said. "But I only joined because I was looking for you, too! I didn't know how to **go to the Overworld** and was too scared to go there alone."

I felt **so relieved.** Of course. I knew Clyde wouldn't **actually** join them.

"We have to **get out of here,**" I said. "Everyone keeps **freaking out** when they see me."

Clyde nodded. "**I'll say!** A blaze just flew past me, **upside down!**"

We heard a faint boom off in the distance, as though the blaze had **crashed into a wall** and **exploded.**

Batwing **winced.** "**Poor guy.** Anyway, let's get out of here. More monsters will show up **any minute.**"

"He's right," Clyde said. "**Let's go.**"

Long story short, I finally **caught up** with Clyde again. We made it out of the nether fortress **without much trouble.**

"The Overworld is in **danger**," Clyde said, once we were **in the clear.** "EnderStar is gearing up for something **big**. Much bigger than we thought. **Not even the Nether** will be safe."

"About that," Batwing said. "You two seem like **cool** mobs. I'd like to **introduce you** to my friends."

"**Fine by me**," I said. "As long as they won't do something crazy upon seeing me like turn into **a baby slime**."

I didn't know it then, but Batwing was about to show us what I now consider to be **the coolest place** in the Nether.

During our trip to see Batwing's friends, the wither skeleton did something **strange.** He retrieved **a purple rock** from somewhere I couldn't see.

"That's **a strange-looking rock**," I said.

"It's not a rock. **It's a crystal.** And it's called a **tellstone**."

"What does it do?"

"It can be used to **send messages** to other people. Even people who are **far away.** Even people you don't really know. You can speak with them **in their dreams.**"

"How is that possible?"

"I don't know. **Magic.** Anyway, it isn't working properly. I was only able to **contact two villagers.**"

"Can we speak to them now?" I asked.

"Hmm . . . maybe. **Let's try.**"

Batwing held the crystal closer so that I could see.

"**Nah.** Maybe they're not sleeping right now. . . . **Oh, wait!** Guess they are."

The face of **a villager boy** appeared in the crystal. It was **the strangest thing** I'd ever seen.

The villager's voice seemed to resound from **within** the tellstone:

"As if **my dreams** aren't bad enough. Now I get to listen to **this bonehead** talk in that scratchy, gravelly voice of his."

Batwing moved the crystal closer and began speaking into it.

"**Bonehead?** I'm not the one who just bombed **three tests!** Hey, I'm sorry, **all right?** Hey! Don't shut me out, kid! Look, I'm not going to ask you to save me! **Someone else already did!**"

Then the wither skeleton extended his arm to move the crystal farther away from us.

When he did, the villager boy seemed **shocked.** It was like he really could **see me** somehow.

"Don't look at them like **that!**" Batwing said, speaking into the crystal once more. "They're not monsters! Well, **okay,** they **are** monsters, and so am I, but **we're good!** We're not like the rest! We've made **a whole city** by ourselves! A city of good monsters, hidden from all **the bad ones!** By the way, this is **Eeebs.** He won't bite. **Promise!** Oh, and that's Clyde over there. **Both of them are really nice!**"

He said a lot more to the villager *(advice of some kind)*, but I've already forgotten it.

SUNDAY—UPDATE VII

After walking across **countless** hills and following Batwing through an enormous cave, I finally saw it:

Lavacrest.

The city of **good monsters,** hidden **deep** within a netherrack mountain.

Vast streets of nether brick **stretched endlessly.** Blocks of **glowstone** sat upon posts of nether-brick fence. Countless **iron doors** led to **shops,** homes, and even **schools** where monsters could study **various crafts,** like mining and **enchanting.**

Every monster **imaginable** could be seen here, even some not native to **this dimension,** such as **endermen** and **witches.** They had traveled here to learn more about **magic.** Magic . . . that was something I was totally unaware of, **until today.**

Witches, **huddled in groups** outside, were uttering strange words. **White glyphs** hovered in the air before them.

"What are they doing?" I asked.

"Casting a **protective spell,**" Batwing said. "I forgot the name."

"**Reinforce,**" Clyde said. "They're enchanting the city's blocks to be **more resistant** to explosions."

"There's even a spell that can make a block **impossible to mine,**" Batwing said. "It's pretty **high-level,** though, and consumes **a diamond** upon casting."

As we **wandered** the streets, with me staring in awe, Clyde and Batwing went on about the many **block enchantment spells.** One spell, **Spike Growth,** caused a block to grow spikes on each of its sides, **damaging** anyone touching it or walking across its surface—much like **cactus. First Burst** acted like **a trap:** Anyone stepping on it **caught fire.** There was also a lightning-based version, known simply as **Zap.** Another, **Frost Aura,** provided a **slowing effect.**

"Kind of like **soul sand,**" Clyde said. "Except it also makes you attack slower."

"**Soul sand?**"

Batwing sighed. "That **sand** you saw in the nether fortress."

In addition to block enchantment spells there were spells that created new types of blocks, such as **Shadow Block.** After casting this spell, you chose a **material**—sand, cobblestone, netherrack, anything—and **a block of that type** would appear. This block, although **appearing real** in every way, was something called an **"illusion."** You could **walk through it** as easily as walking through air.

"We're about to place these blocks across **the cave entrance** leading to this city," Batwing said. "That way, EnderStar's **soldiers** will **never find** this place."

"Don't you need **a bat's wing** to cast that one?" Clyde asked.

Batwing nodded. "**Yeah.** We really need to head to the Overworld and go **bat hunting.**"

Another spell was called **"Light Block."** It created a block of **intense** white light, which could be walked through. However, standing within such a block was like standing in **sunlight.**

A more powerful version of the spell, **Concentrated Light Block,** was **twice the normal strength** of sunlight, meaning it would burn monsters to **a crisp.**

"We figure a wall of light blocks might be **useful** against a zombie horde," Batwing said. "Sadly, both versions of Light Block require **emeralds** to cast."

And then there was **Mud Aspect,** which gave a block **mud-like** consistency. Anyone stepping into it would slowly **sink down.** Their movement speed would be **decreased** as well, although not as much as the effect Frost Aura provided.

Needless to say, **Slime Aspect** gave any block the properties of **slime,** meaning it could be used to **bounce upward.**

But the **most interesting,** in my opinion, was **Teleporter Cube.** I didn't understand how it worked, but Clyde said it could be used to **travel** vast distances **instantaneously.**

"Not a single monster in the city knows that spell," Batwing said. "Not even Greyfellow."

I blinked. "**Greyfellow?**"

For once, Batwing **wasn't annoyed** at my cluelessness. "He's the guy who **runs** this place."

"He's also the guy we're **going to see,**" Clyde added. "I'm sure he must know more about your . . . **current state.**"

Perhaps ten minutes later, we reached **Greyfellow's** home: a huge hut made of **nether quartz.** Batwing increased his pace, muttering something to himself.

Clyde and I exchanged glances
and followed him in.

Greyfellow was an enderman.

He wasn't black, however, but **light gray** in color with bright **sky-blue eyes.** In addition, he wore a fancy-looking **white hat,** not unlike those typically worn by witches. He's known as an **"endermage,"** one of the last **enderman wizards** in all of Minecraftia.

"Where have you been?" he said to Batwing.

"Yeah, about that," Batwing said.

"Those bums stranded me out there."

"Oh?"

Batwing withdrew **the brilliant purple tellstone** from his inventory. "And your little **crystal** didn't work."

"What do you mean **it didn't work?**"

"Well, I tried telling **those villagers** that the Overworld is in danger. I **begged** them to set me free. **The girl** just **ignored** me, and **this little punk, Runt,** kept telling me to go away."

"My apologies," Greyfellow said. "Villagers are a **crude** folk. They can sometimes be . . . **uncouth.** Interesting that you weren't able to contact **anyone else,** though. Hmm . . . Give me **the tellstone.**"

"**Gladly.** Take it."

"I shall craft you **a new one** later tonight," the endermage said. He glanced at Clyde and me. "And who are **your new friends?**"

Batwing introduced us, and the endermage noticed **my mark.** "**Interesting.** You come from the Overworld, then? **Yes.** You were once **a kitten.** I can see that now."

"Do you know what happened to me?" I asked.

"**I believe so.** Although, I must consult the **ancient texts.** Go now. **Eat. Sleep.** In the morning, we shall speak again."

Before long, I'd eaten **three cooked salmon** and was **curled up** next to a burning block of netherrack. How these monsters got ahold of **salmon,** I didn't know and didn't ask.

Magic, **probably.**

Yawn. Maybe they can conjure food as well as blocks?

As I dozed off,
I started <u>purring</u>.

That morning, I met up with the **gray enderman** again. He told me a lot of stuff and showed me this **huge, ancient book.**

He let me **borrow it,** so I'm going to copy some of it down.

***

THE PROPHECY OF MINECRAFTIA, VOLUME I

And so shall it be: In these perilous times, two Saviors shall descend from the Sacred Light and drive the Veil of Darkness to each corner of the world.

One Savior shall take the form of a young Human man—KOLB. He represents all that is Earthly and Known. The other shall arrive in the form of a young Sylph woman of most enchanting beauty—IONE. She represents the Unearthly, the Unknown.

Alas, our Saviors walk a difficult path, for their Divine Weapons, forged by the White Shepherd and blessed with Sacred Light, were all but destroyed during the Second War. Only when their shards have been reunited can each Weapon be fully re-forged.

In addition to our Saviors, five Beings shall be Chosen by the Light:

1.) A villager displaying incredible creativity and insight, with compassion for all life. He shall take up the sword and become not only a Warrior but a supreme Tactician without equal. Although his power comes from within, the Sacred Light shall assist him in the form of Luck. He is a champion of the Overworld.

2.) Three animals displaying the highest bravery in the face of great danger and loyalty to their friends. The gender and form of each animal are Unknown. They shall be blessed with higher intelligence and begin to take on the aspects of monsters. The first of these Chosen Animals shall seek to meet and serve the first Chosen Being. These animals are champions of the Nether.

3.) The third Chosen Being is entirely Unknown, although it is Known that this Being shall be most bizarre in nature. He serves as a champion of the End.

Know this: As the Darkness continues to spread across our World, our Saviors must seek to reclaim the fragments of their Divine Weapons, for these blades are the only two Divine Weapons remaining after the Second War. The rest, destroyed by the Eyeless One, are lost for eternity.

Before all else, our Saviors shall head to the Capital of our World, known as Aetheria City, where they shall learn of past knowledge and train themselves, for their energy will have diminished during their journey.

Soon thereafter, the Great War shall begin between the forces of Light and Darkness.

***

Okay. There's **much more** to that book, but my head hurts. *(My paw, too.)*

In dark times, heroes from "**another world**" will arrive to **fight** against evil. Five beings from this world have been **selected** as well.

I'm **one of the animals** mentioned. I'm supposed to find and serve the first "**Chosen Being**." A villager. That means I need to return to **the Overworld**.

But that enderman wizard, **Greyfellow,** doesn't want me to. Not yet. He says I must learn more about **my abilities** before I leave. I must become **stronger**.

We talked about this stuff **all day.** I'm really **tired,** now. Talking in **a non-cat language** I've just learned is still difficult for me, remember?

By the way, some of the monsters here **really can** conjure food with magic. **It's so cool.** All I **have to do** is **ask** some witch or enderman for raw salmon. I can **cook it** myself because I've been blessed with **higher intelligence,** according to that old book. **How cool is** that?! **Meow!**

Time for sleep.
My "training" starts tomorrow.

"They've found us! They've found us!"

I woke up to **a creeper wizard** shouting these words. I was still at **Greyfellow's** house. When I walked outside, I saw so many different monsters **running around** and shouting.

From this crowd, Greyfellow and Batwing **emerged.** They were holding on to a zombie pigman by each arm. He seemed familiar somehow. But where could I have **seen him before?**

"We found him **sneaking around** just outside the city!" Batwing said. **"Little snoop!"**

Clyde floated down to our level. "What are we going to do with him?"

"We'll have to **imprison him,**" Greyfellow said. "If we let him go, he'll give EnderStar **the location** of our city."

"N-no," the pigman said. **"Me. Want. T-to—"**

"Shut it!" Batwing said. "You'll say anything to get away!"

A creeper shouted: **"Hisssss, me blow him up!"**

"I say we **throw him** into the **pit!**" a nearby witch shouted. **"That's the best way!"**

"Yesh! Duh pit! **Duh pit!"** After uttering these noises, several zombie pigmen *(good ones, apparently?)* began chanting: **"Duh pit! Duh pit! Duh pit!"**

111

Soon, hundreds of monsters joined in.

(However, most were shouting/chanting "the pit" as opposed to "duh pit." Why do some speak differently?)

"They're **right**," Batwing said. "There's only one way we **deal with** our enemies, and that's tossing them in **the pit.** A good dropkick from behind—not too hard, eh, a little encouraging tap in the rear—and **boom**, one-way ticket to another dimension. Suddenly, our problem is **no longer our** problem, just **breakfast** for some hungry **Void beast.**"

A tear ran down Clyde's cheek. He spun around. "**No!** What are you saying?! **We can't do that!** If we do, we'll be just as bad as EnderStar!" He paused. "Wait. **Um . . . guys?** What's **the pit?**"

"Oh. Okay. So that's the pit."

Some say it goes on **forever,** but Greyfellow told me the truth: **It actually reaches the Void.**

113

When you fall in, you'll fall for **quite a long way.** But after some **6,570 blocks,** you'll eventually arrive in **a bizarre world.** A world of **eternal night** containing **crystalline** plants, lakes of **glowing blue ooze, invisible** things brushing past you and **whispering** into your ear, and, yes, **horrifying** monsters.

At least, that's what **Greyfellow** told me when I asked him about it. Maybe he's just **trying to scare me?**

He also said **a race of peaceful** mushroom people live there, who know about such things as **"advanced crafting"** and **"advanced brewing."** Whatever **that** means.

Anyway, **thirty minutes** later, over one thousand monsters were standing around this seemingly **bottomless hole** that may or may not have led to a place **one thousand times crazier** than the Nether.

The **prisoner** was standing on the very edge, his back turned to us. Batwing was right behind him.

"Just **say the word,** Greyfellow, and I'll dropkick this **punk** into a **brand-new dimension!"**

"P-please," the pigman said. "Me. No. B-b-b . . . b . . . b-bad."

The endermage closed his eyes for what must have been **several minutes.**

Ghast tears were **running down** Clyde's cheeks, and two witches were now trying to **collect them.**

I stared at the pigman the whole time. *Now where have I seen him before? That thing on his head.* I saw a pigman wearing one of those before.

Wait a second! He was the guy leading all the other monsters in the Overworld after EnderStar teleported away. He was the **smart one**, the zombie pigman who could actually talk.

What's his name again?

Rarg? Yes! **Rarg**, the zombie pigman captain!

"Very well," Greyfellow said at last. "I have decided that—"

"**No!**" I shouted. I walked up to Rarg and turned to the other monsters. "**Wait!** I've seen this pigman before!"

"**What?** In the nether fortress?" Batwing said. "So what?"

"In **the Overworld**," I said. "I watched from a distance as EnderStar's army **panicked, blinded** by sunlight. They had no idea **how bright** the sun can be."

"What's your point?" Greyfellow said.

"Well, while I was watching them, I sensed **something good** in this pigman. Since he was wearing **that thing** on his head, he was **the only one** who wasn't blinded. He helped his fellow monsters return to the Nether by **singing a song** so that they could follow him."

The endermage nodded. "I see, I see. **Hmm** . . . wearing a helmet, **yes.** So, he's quite **smart.** Hmm."

"Not only that," I said, "I could somehow **sense** that he didn't **want** to be there. Didn't want any part of attacking the Overworld. He kept **hesitating** whenever EnderStar spoke to him."

"**C'mon!**" Batwing said. "You know we can't do anything but give this guy **a good kick!** He'll give away our **location** if we don't!"

"**Quiet,**" Greyfellow said. He walked up to Rarg. "Pigman. **Is it true?** Do you really wish to **abandon** EnderStar's army and join us?"

"**Y-yes,**" Rarg said. "Me **tired** of **boss man.** And me have many friends also tired of boss man. Boss man **always screaming.** Always want us do **bad thing.** We don't want do bad thing."

"Then why didn't you leave **before?**" Greyfellow asked.

"**We scared.** Boss man **make fire** from no fire. Boss man make **white zap light** from no white zap light. Boss man also turn three me friend into **flying black squeaky thing.** Then he **eat** flying black squeaky thing. **Me SO sad.** Me so **angry.** When me see flying black squeaky thing . . . **me remember. Me cry.** Me want help beat him."

"Flying black squeaky thing?" Batwing facepalmed. "This is like talking to that kitten! **Can you make sense, please?**"

"He means **bats,**" I said.

"Oh. Right."

"I'm no wizard, but I believe there's only one spell that can **turn someone into a bat,**" Clyde said.

116

"Yes." Greyfellow's expression grew even **more serious.** **Polymorph III.** This is **bad news** indeed. He's **much more powerful** than we thought."

"Why don't we let Rarg **join us,** then?" Clyde asked. "If he really does **want out** of EnderStar's army, he can tell us **everything** he knows!"

"**Not a bad idea,**" Greyfellow said. "He may also **convince** his friends to switch sides and join us."

Batwing **facepalmed** again. "Man, don't you guys know **anything? **We can't take **any chances!** Listen, I'm a wither skeleton, okay? I grew up in that nether fortress. I used to be a **bad mob.** I know what bad mobs think. And here's what bad mobs think: **bad things.** EnderStar probably sent him here and told him to **say all of that stuff.** And, once we finally start **trusting** him and let him stay here and feed him **mushrooms** and **slimeball stew** and the many other **nasty** things his kind eats, he'll learn everything about us, go back to the nether fortress, and **squeal** like a . . . um . . . pigman?"

The other monsters seemed **divided.** Some nodded their heads in agreement with Greyfellow and Clyde, and others were thinking along the same lines as Batwing. It was a situation **stickier** than any slime.

Then Rarg held out **a stack of ender pearls.** "Me. G-g-g . . . g-g . . ."

"**Give?**" I asked.

"Y-yes. **Me g-give.**"

"W-where did you get those?!" Batwing cried out.

"Me grab **green things.** From big red house. Me g-g . . . give you. **Okay?**"

"**Interesting,**" Greyfellow said, taking the stack of ender pearls. "First the kitten, and now **this.**"

Rarg then held out a stack of **gold bars.** "Shiny thing. Me also take these. Boss man shiny pile. Boss man have **many shiny things** in shiny pile."

He dropped the stack on to the ground, then he retrieved a stack of **shiny green rocks** from his inventory and threw them onto the ground as well. Many monsters **gasped.**

"**So many emeralds!**"

This was followed by at least fifty different glass things filled with water. Although, the water inside wasn't blue but **purple, red, and green. . . .**

"**Potions, too?!**"

"Boss man tell me, **always watch** bottle things. Make sure no monster take bottle things. Why bottle things so important? Me wonder. But secret. Me try drinking bottle thing once. Me **jump very high.**" He chuckled. "Me **like** bottle things."

An **unbelievable** amount of items formed a pile at Rarg's big boots.

There were several books, like the one I'm currently writing in. Except, they **shimmered purple.** Was that due to magic?

"Enchanting books?!" a few monsters exclaimed.

Rarg also threw down a pile of **shiny whitish-blue rocks.** Those are called **diamonds,** apparently.

"Boss man say shiny rock **most good,**" Rarg said. "No eat shiny rock. Shiny rock hard. But shiny rock make good stab thing. Shiny rock also make good **body thing,** like on head or feet."

Around me, **the excitement** of the other monsters **filled the air.** They kept chattering away about emeralds, diamonds, enchanted books, potions. . . .

"Okay. Very last thing. **Shiny metal.** I find in wood box. Boss man say this **junk.** But me think **so pretty.**"

Rarg the zombie pigman withdrew another rock from his inventory. Wait, **no?** It wasn't a rock. **It was a piece of metal?** It was **bright silver** and shimmered **many different colors.** It was **so beautiful.** The most common color by far was this **dazzling shade of green.**

"**Unbelievable,**" Greyfellow said. "I don't believe . . . **this is . . .** quite surely, **it can't be.** . . . My fellow monsters, we are looking at **a shard. One of the seven shards of Critbringer.**"

Everyone fell **silent,** and then:

"Huh?"

"Shard?"

"**Critbringer?**"

"What are you talking about, Greyfellow?"

"It looks like **a piece of metal** to me."

"It is a piece of metal," Greyfellow said. "But not iron. **That is adamant,** a metal **so rare** in our time that it was thought to exist **only in legend.**"

I remembered the old book Greyfellow had let me borrow.

. . . Divine Weapons . . . all but destroyed during the Second War. Only when their shards have been reunited can each Weapon be fully re-forged. . . .

"You mean, this is from one of the sharp sticks mentioned in the book?" I said. "**The swords,** I mean."

"**Exactly!**" Greyfellow said.

The other monsters didn't seem to **understand.** They looked at each other with total **confusion** in their square eyes.

The gray enderman scowled at them. "**Fools!** Have none of you read of **the Prophecy?!** This piece of metal is **a fragment from the legendary sword Critbringer!** A sword forged in ancient times, when monsters **far more powerful** than any of you roamed in great number! Back then, weapons had to be strong enough for **land wyrms, lurkers,** and other **horrific** beasts you cannot possibly imagine! This is one of the only weapons still in existence **powerful enough to** harm **the Eyeless One,** whose real name I shall not utter here!"

"Lurkers?" Batwing sighed. "Are those the giant black squid-like things with **one thousand tentacles** and a single huge purple eye? The ones that live deep underground? The reason why certain mineshafts are abandoned? The monsters that reduce the **durability** of your items with a single glance? I thought those things were just **a legend**." He shrugged. "Huh. Who knew?"

"**Fool!**" Greyfellow grabbed **the shard** and turned to Rarg. "I can see now that **destiny** has brought you to us."

The enderman addressed the entire crowd: "No harm shall come to this pigman! **Free him at once** and see to it that he is **introduced** to our city!" He sighed. "I **must go** now. I have much work to do. **Kitten, come.**"

Rarg turned to me. "Thank you, **blue fuzz thing.** You help me. **Me so happy.** You me **friend** now?"

"Yes," I said to Rarg. "**Me you friend now.**"

"Breathe!" the endermage shouted. "**Breathe!!**"

"I'm **breathing**," I said. "**I'm breathing!** But as you can see, **your Grand High Endermage-ness**, no fireballs are coming out!"

"Try harder!"

Breathe, **breathe, breathe.**

Nothing. Just little puffs of air.

We were back at Greyfellow's place. The endermage was trying to teach me how to use **monster abilities.**

As I exhaled **over and over**, a non-zombified pigman who stood nearby saw me and started doing the same. Moments later: "**O'gorg!** Me pants-pants **heavy** now. I go **bathroom** now-now."

"**Leave us at once!**" the endermage shouted. The pigman left. "Clyde! **Clyde!** Oh, where did that silly ghast run off to?!"

"**I'm here!**" the ghast called out. "What's **the problem?**"

"Do you see that **wall of obsidian?**" Greyfellow asked. "Breathe **a fireball** on it!"

"Can you stop shouting?"

"**Now!!**"

As commanded, the ghast drew in a deep breath, and—**whoosh!**—spit out a large **fireball.** It hit the obsidian wall nearby without any real effect.

122

"Now do it **again! Keep doing it!**"

One after another, I watched Clyde spit fireballs at the obsidian wall.

"**Good!**" the enderman said. "Now, kitten. **You try.**"

"Sure thing."

Breathe! **Breathe! Breathe!**

Pretty pathetic. Not even a **puff** of smoke.

"You aren't trying hard enough!" Greyfellow shouted. "**Try!!**"

"I **am** trying!" I shouted.

"**Try harder!!**"

"**I am!!**"

"There's a large chance your homeworld is going to be **destroyed,** kitten! **Do you understand?!**"

I hissed. "Hey! Stop freaking out, okay?! For the past hour it's been '**Jump here! Swim** in that lava **over there!** Go **invisible!** Magically **spit out fireballs** as if you're a—'"

Suddenly, my whole body shook.

Cough, hack.
Ahackckahackahack.
Hackhackhackackackkkkkkkkk.

What's wrong with me? **This is so painful!** It's like coughing up **a hairball** but ten times worse!

I coughed up **a fireball** instead. It was a **tiny** thing, maybe ten times the size of a spark. It flew out of my mouth and **wobbled** through the air. There was a sad little sound as it did: **p'tweeeeeeeeeeee. . . .**

This tiny fireball, flying **so slowly** *(slower than a zombie pigman walking)* slowed down even more the more it flew toward the wall. It continued making that little noise: **eeeee. . . .**

We **all watched** as it continued to fly forward **pathetically.** It **literally** took twenty seconds to travel a distance of **nine blocks.** Finally, there was a slight sputtering sound as it hit the wall and vanished.

I coughed **again.** A little puff of smoke came out. For a long time afterward: **silence.**

I looked at **Clyde.** Clyde looked at **the enderman.** The enderman looked at **me.** I looked at **the enderman.** The enderman looked at **Clyde.** Clyde looked at **me.** Then we **all** looked at the small obsidian wall **my tiny little fireball** had struck.

"I don't believe it," Greyfellow said. "**The Prophecy! It really is true!**"

Clyde started spinning around **frantically.** "**So cool,** Eeebs! **Wow!** I knew you could do it!"

"Yeah, yeah, **not bad, kid!**" Batwing was standing in the doorway, now. "So, you're **some kind of mutant,** huh?"

Moments later, I heard **a familiar voice.** A **girl's** voice. Most of all, it was **the voice of a kitten.** "Hey?! **Eeebs?!** What was **that?!**"

Tufty and **Meowz** were also standing in the doorway. **My friends from the Overworld.** Strangely, although I recognized them, they no longer looked like kittens. **Not really.**

Big claws.
Ridiculously long ears.
As a matter of fact, and, as **strange** as it sounds,
well . . . **they almost kind of looked like me.**

Yesterday, I breathed fire.

At the same time, my friends showed up, Tufty and Meowz. They were pretty much in the same boat as I was several days ago: clueless.

They still resembled their former selves. Tufty was still orange-ish. Meowz was still mostly white. However, they looked scary now. Like an-enderman-staring-at-you-in-a-totally-dark-room-making-weird-little-noises-with-only-its-glowing-purple-eyes-being-visible scary. Actually, worse than that. Like my-mom-calling-me-by-my-full-name-and-threatening-to-make-me-eat-pufferfish-casserole-for-a-week scary or human-trying-to-tame-me-with-a-pumpkin-instead-of-a-fish scary.

Meowz crept into the house. "Eeebs?"

Tufty followed her in with his tail between his legs.

The endermage, Greyfellow, nearly fainted upon seeing them. He turned to Batwing. "I can't . . . I don't . . . what is happening, Batwing? Yesterday, everything was so normal. I was drinking some redstone tea, thinking about what to craft. Then this kitten shows up with the mark. Then a zombie pigman not only joins our side but hands over EnderStar's treasure horde. Then, the kitten actually breathes fire. I'd never believed in the Prophecy myself!

Did you? And now two of his friends arrive, apparently **Chosen** as well. . . ."

He **trailed off** and appeared to be looking at something far away.

Batwing sighed. "Three kittens as **Chosen Animals.** Why couldn't it have been something way **more crazy,** like a chicken and a donkey? A bat and a cow?"

"I was hoping for a squid and a pig!" Clyde said. "I read about **squids,** once."

"Anything but **three kittens.**" The wither skeleton nudged **Greyfellow.**

The endermage mumbled absently, still **staring** ahead: "I like redstone tea . . . and . . . **kittens . . . three** kittens . . . what does it **mean . . . ?**"

"So, these are **your friends,** Eeebs?" Clyde **smiled.** Well, he didn't, really, but he **didn't sniffle** or anything like that, and his frown vanished. That's **pretty much** like smiling for a ghast.

"**Yes,**" I said, approaching Tufty and Meowz.

"We came across **the witch,**" Meowz said. "She told us everything."

"We didn't believe her when she said we could use **the abilities of monsters,**" Tufty said. "**It's true,** though. This is so **cool!** How can I breathe fire like that?"

"You guys really shouldn't have followed me," I said. "**Really.** You don't know what you've gotten yourselves **into.**"

Meowz looked like she was about to cry. "Eebs?"

"Yeah."

"What's happening?"

"About that, purrrr . . ."

I tried telling them about the Prophecy, and I showed them Greyfellow's book. It was hard for me to explain everything to them, and the endermage wouldn't chime in and help me out. He just kept babbling on about redstone tea: how he liked it warm although not too warm, how he added some crushed flower petals like blue orchids to the recipe to make it taste better, how he thought it further improved the taste and added "more kick" when he made it using a brewing stand instead of a crafting table. . . .

I turned to the endermage. "Hey? Greyfellow? Who wrote this book, anyway?"

". . . it's the bubbling process," he mumbled. "A brewing stand aerates the tea, providing a more crisp and refreshing flavor. . . ."

My ears and tail lowered, I started thinking that after learning how to spit fireballs, my next power was going to be to shoot smoke out of my ears.

"Right," I said. "Forget about who wrote it, then. What I really mean to ask is, how did they know all of this stuff was going to happen? How did they know three animals would be changed?"

Greyfellow nodded. "Why, yes . . . **pink tulip** certainly tastes better than **oxeye daisy,** yes . . . yes, indeed. . . ."

"**Um,** what's wrong with him?" Batwing said.

Clyde **shrugged.** Well, Clyde has no shoulders—he's just a giant white block with a face, really—but, anyway, for some reason **I felt** that he shrugged. "**Too much** has happened today."

"You could say that." The wither skeleton glanced out the window. "I'll go check on **Rarg** and see if he's okay. Listen, Eeebs. Why don't you hold off on telling your friends about **the Prophecy** till our endermage friend here isn't **bumbling around** like a **land squid?** In the meantime, you can show your friends **around the city.** Cool?"

"**Sure,**" I said, glancing at the two nether kittens. "Shall we?"

The three of us left Greyfellow's hut. I didn't **freak out** at the sight of my friends, not even then. I was still **so shocked** by everything. I was about to join the endermage. If just **one more** crazy thing had happened, I'd have started mumbling about **pufferfish cookies:** how to align the eggs, milk, and sugar **pixel** by **pixel** on the crafting table in a purrfect way to achieve a five-star rating from the **International Minecraftian Baker's Society,** in not only **consistency** but also **form** and texture, the **lightness** of the bread, **crisp** yet never crumbling, with each tiny cube of sugar and baked pufferfish spread evenly throughout the biscuits to achieve a pastry both **magnificent** to the eye and simply **bursting with flavor.**

129

But then I wasn't sure if the **International Minecraftian Baker's Society** had such a **refined** taste as a nether kitten's, and soon I began to wonder whether any of them would appreciate the **elegance** of a cookie made of equal parts sugar and fish.

Speaking of **Greyfellow**.

(Wait . . . . I wasn't speaking of him. Whatever.)

Anyway, here are a few drawings of **his house.**

Easy to guess
that an enderman
lives here.

131

Well, I showed my friends around **Good Mob City.** We didn't **talk** much, though. They were **just as silent** as me.

I mean, all of this stuff has happened **SO** fast. Just a week ago, we were playing **hide-and-seek.** Now, we're nothing like our former selves. We're supposed to help **save the world.**

An hour or so later we headed back to the gray enderman. He'd **finally calmed down** a little.

"Sorry about that," he said. "I just couldn't believe it. Still can't. **The Prophecy** really is **true?!** Which means . . . our world is going to suffer through yet **another Great War.**"

"What are we supposed to do?" I asked, getting **straight to the point.**

"**Hmm.** First, let's try something. Kittens, I want you to think about the word **'ability.'** Or just **imagine** your abilities in general. Picture them in your **mind.**"

Tufty must have thought of his abilities first.

Seconds after the endermage spoke, **a gray screen** appeared before the orange nether kitten. This screen was **completely flat,** two-dimensional, and seemed to be made out of **colored light.**

"**Wow!**" Meowz waved a paw through Tufty's screen, and it **passed through** without any resistance. "What **is** that thing?"

"Those screens are called visual **enchantments**," the enderman said. "They can be used to **interact** with objects or your **inventory**, or they can simply **display data**."

"And what are **abilities?**" Tufty asked.

"All monsters have abilities," Greyfellow said. "Creepers **move silently**. Endermen **teleport**. Zombies **break down doors**. Of course, you kittens have **more abilities** than any normal mob."

I tried to concentrate on the word "ability."
A screen appeared before me as well.

ABILITIES

OBSIDIAN FUR
HIGHER INTELLIGENCE
PIGMAN FRENZY
ASPECT OF THE SPIDER
GHAST FIREBALL
CREEP
FIRE AFFINITY
PACK BEAST

The enderman then **told us** that we could either **touch** an ability's name on the screen or **focus on it** with our mind to access **another screen.** This screen would tell us more about **that specific ability.**

When I batted at the words "Obsidian Fur" with a paw, the words upon the screen **changed** to:

ABILITY:
OBSIDIAN FUR
LEVEL: ■□□□□□□□□
TYPE: MONSTER, PASSIVE

Your fur has become exceedingly dense and tough, making you more resistant to damage. For each level of this ability, your armor is increased slightly and all critical hits will deal 5% less damage (50% maximum).

"If you want to go back to the **first screen,**" Greyfellow said, "just concentrate on that word. 'Back.' Or you could speak it **out loud.**"

I tried the latter. "**Back.**"

The visual enchantment screen returned to its former state.

"Interesting." Touching the screen with her paws, Meowz began **browsing through** all of her abilities.

I did the same, pawing down the list, accessing each **sub-menu,** reading it, and saying the word **"back"** in my mind each time.

Here's a **full list** of my abilities:

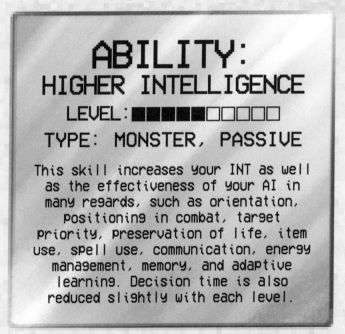

ABILITY:
HIGHER INTELLIGENCE
LEVEL: ■■■■■■□□□□□
TYPE: MONSTER, PASSIVE

This skill increases your INT as well as the effectiveness of your AI in many regards, such as orientation, positioning in combat, target priority, preservation of life, item use, spell use, communication, energy management, memory, and adaptive learning. Decision time is also reduced slightly with each level.

*(I'm guessing "INT" means **intelligence?** I have no idea what "AI" means and neither does Greyfellow.)*

ABILITY:
PIGMAN FRENZY
LEVEL: ■■■□□□□□□□
TYPE: MONSTER, PASSIVE,
ACTIVATED

Passively increases your base
movement, sprinting, crouching,
and swimming speeds. Additionally,
you may activate this ability to
ignore any slow debuff for a short
amount of time (1 second/level),
such as that caused by walking
through cobwebs or soul sand.

ABILITY:
ASPECT OF THE SPIDER
LEVEL: ■□□□□□□□□□
TYPE: MONSTER, PASSIVE

You can move vertically up and down
walls as though they were ladders.

ABILITY:
GHAST FIREBALL

LEVEL: ■□□□□□□□□□

TYPE: MONSTER,
ACTIVE (75 ENERGY)

You can breathe fire! Each level increases the fireball's damage and velocity and reduces the energy cost by 2.

ABILITY:
CREEP

LEVEL: ■■□□□□□□□□

TYPE: MONSTER, PASSIVE

You move as silently as a creeper. While standing still, you will gain camouflage, which increases with level, resulting in almost complete invisibility once mastered.

ABILITY:
FIRE AFFINITY
LEVEL: ■■■■■■■■■■■
TYPE: MONSTER, PASSIVE

You've mastered this skill!
You are immune to the effects
of both fire and lava.

ABILITY:
PACK BEAST
LEVEL: ■■■□□□□□□□□
TYPE: MONSTER, PASSIVE

You gain one additional inventory
slot with each level of this skill.

The endermage said an ability's **level** is a measure of how **powerful** it is. So, most of my abilities are still **pretty weak.** But they won't be like that **forever!**

"By the way, **energy is used** for abilities," the enderman said. **"Spells,** too. Using abilities and casting spells **drain your energy bar.** That's why Eeebs could breathe **only one** fireball yesterday and only puffs of smoke afterward. Energy **slowly recharges** over time. So it's best to use your abilities **only** when you **absolutely need them.** Like most monsters, you have a maximum of **100 energy."**

"How do we know how much energy we currently have?" Tufty asked.

"That's **the yellow bar** in your HUD, or **heads-up display.** Simply concentrate upon the word 'HUD' in your mind, and it will appear across the bottom of **your vision.** If you are injured, hungry, drained of energy, or debuffed in any way, your HUD will **automatically** appear, as a kind of reminder, until your condition **improves."**

Okay, let's try it: <u>HUD</u>.

As soon as I thought this, a **bunch of stuff** appeared across the bottom of my vision, just like the enderman had described.

"The hearts are a measure of your **life force**," Greyfellow said. "Each heart represents **two hit points.** By the way, I'm curious. How many hearts do you have?"

Each of us replied with the same number:

"**Ten!**"

"**Twenty hit points,** then. **Not much.** You'll gain much more as you **grow stronger,** though."

"What about the **gray shirt things?**" I asked, not wanting to think about what would happen if all of my hearts were **removed.**

"That's a visual indicator of your **protection,** otherwise known as **armor.** The more armor you have, the **less damage** you will take. Some forms of damage bypass armor, however."

"How about **the boxes?**"

"Your **hotbar.** You can secure items to your body—with the help of a **belt,** for example—or in an easy-to-reach location in your **inventory.** You may then access those items **quickly.**"

All three nether kittens exchanged glances: "**Inventory?**"

140

The enderman then explained how we each have an "extra-dimensional space" that lets us carry many items. We only have to say "inventory" in our minds for the inventory screen to appear. That must be how Batwing withdrew the tellstone from what looked like thin air: He accessed his inventory.

"Your inventories are currently quite small," Greyfellow said. "You can increase the size of your inventory by wearing a container, like a belt pouch. There are even enchanted containers that dramatically increase your inventory space. Sadly, such items, enchanted or not, won't be easy for kittens to wear. They aren't normally designed for animals. An easy way around that, if you felt the need to carry many items, would be to level-up your Pack Beast ability."

Tufty blinked. "Um, can you repeat that? I'm totally confused."

"Same here," I said. "I guess that means we really need to level-up our Higher Intelligence ability, huh?"

After we **played around** with our **visual enchantment screens,**
a question spawned in my mind. "Say, how do we **get stronger,**
anyway? And how can our abilities gain **levels?**"

The enderman gave me a **strange** look. All of his expressions were
strange, really, but his expression then was as if I'd just asked why
zombie pigmen are purple and have **ice cream cones** for heads.

"By doing **your job,**" he said.

"And that is?"

"Turning **Herobrine's** and **EnderStar's minions** into clouds of
smoke. Every time you **defeat** one, you'll absorb some of its power. Of
course, you'll also grow stronger by **questing.**"

Questing . . . ?

Before anyone could even ask for clarification, **more screens**
appeared before us.

Like with the ability screens, simply thinking about the word **"quest"**
conjured what could be called a **"quest screen":**

ACTIVE QUEST:
SERVING YOUR MASTERS

Your destiny awaits! Go now,
nether kitten, and find the
villager you are meant to serve!

Sadly, Tufty and Meowz had different messages on their quest

screens.

ACTIVE QUEST:
SURPRISE ATTACK!

You must remain in the city of
Lavacrest. Here, you will further
improve your abilities and take part
in a siege upon the nether fortress!

"What does all of this **mean?!**" Tufty said. "It's so **weird!**"

"I have to agree," Meowz said. "I'm **so confused** I could **hiss!** It's not fair, you know? We've been chosen to help **save the world,** and all this new stuff is being thrown at us, and we don't even get **classes** or something?"

"It does seem **an awful lot** has been thrust upon you kittens," Greyfellow said. "**A heavy burden,** indeed. I am doing my best to **teach you,** but there are many things I do not know. Eeebs, I do suggest returning to **the Overworld** as soon as you can. Once there, the first place you should head to is **the capital.** Ask around for the **Library.** One of **my colleagues** there knows much about **the Prophecy** and may be able to help you locate that **villager.**"

As he said this, I tried **piecing everything together** in my mind.

1.) We're supposed to help fight against **the Eyeless One,** otherwise known as **Herobrine.**

2.) We've been given **abilities,** and we have these things called **quests**—tasks we're supposed to complete.

3.) My first quest is meeting up with that **villager.** A villager I don't know anything about. Is it a boy or a girl? **What's his or her name?** Why do I have to serve that villager, anyway? What, am I just a **pack kitten** or something? I thought **my role** in all this would be a bit more glamorous than that.

"My friends really have to **stay here?**" I asked.

"I believe so. Your quests were **given to you** by **the Immortals** themselves. It would be wise to **follow them.**"

"**That's not fair!**" Meowz said. "I don't want to stay here anymore!"

"**You can't be serious,**" Tufty said. "We can learn more about **our powers!** How **cool** is that? Besides, don't you want to help save the world?"

"Yeah, it's just . . . I already **miss** my family."

"At least you don't have to go into the Overworld alone," I said, "**looking like this.**" I turned to the enderman. "What about Clyde? Can he **go with me?**"

The endermage avoided my gaze. "Well, I . . . **um** . . . it's not exactly written in **the Prophecy.** Plus, I'm not sure whether a ghast could even **survive** in the Overworld for any length of time."

Oh, man.

I didn't want to be **a hero** anymore. **Not without him.**

How could I leave **my best buddy** behind? I'd just caught up with him again!

"There has to be **a way,**" I said. "I really want Clyde to go with me. He's **so smart.** Besides, I know he'll want to."

"It's up to him," Greyfellow said. "I will warn you that **constant exposure** to sunlight could weaken him, possibly even **kill him.**"

145

"Maybe he's **right**," Meowz said. "Once you return to the Overworld, you're going to **scare** enough people as it is. A huge ghast floating behind you certainly won't **help** any."

What will Clyde do once I tell him he **can't go** with me? I thought. Maybe it's for **the best**. The witches seem to like ghast tears, and after I tell Clyde that he can't tag along, their inventories will be **overflowing** with them.

"There's **one more thing** I'd like to try," the enderman said. "**Please follow me.**"

To our **complete amazement,** Greyfellow then whirled around . . . and stepped **into the back wall** of his house!

"Come on! Don't just stand there!"

Tufty and Meowz had **no idea** what was going on. But I'd heard about **shadow blocks** and remembered how you could **walk through them.** In other words, the endermage was taking us to **his secret** chamber.

147

Now, I'd never really met a **wizard** before. At this point, I had no idea that most wizards even had something called **"secret chambers,"** much less how **cool** secret chambers might actually be.

I saw a lot of new stuff today and learned a lot of new words. Such as **"brewing stand."** And **"anvil."** And **"crafting table."** And **"enchantment table."**

and "rune chamber."

"This is called **a rune chamber,**" the enderman said. "Do you know what it does?"

I glanced at the **giant silvery box.** Even though it didn't look all that scary, it **scared me** all the same. "**Errr,** no?"

Tufty wasn't scared, though. He immediately zoomed inside. "Is this like **a house?**" he asked, sniffing the silvery material.

Meowz ran inside as well. "**WOW,**" she said, lifting up her paws, as if the silver material *("iron," I learned later)* was **painful** to the touch.

She left the box as quickly as she'd entered. "It's **freezing** in there!"

"Indeed it is," the enderman said. "It contains a most **powerful** form of magic. Only **three wizards** in all of **Minecraftia** know how to **create** such a device."

"What does it do?" I asked.

"It makes you **stronger,**" he said. "Stronger than you already are, I mean."

Stronger than I already am? Even if I didn't know **how** it made me stronger, it sounded **good** to me. Is there any **downside** to having more super powers? **Basically no.**

"A rune chamber can **permanently** enchant an animal or monster," he said, "granting them additional **strength, defense,** and so on."

"What's **'enchant'?**" Meowz asked.

The enderman shook his head. "Sorry. Not **'enchant.'** Enchanting is more for items, physical objects. The technical term is **'enhance.'** A rune

149

chamber can be used to enhance you. But let's just call it enchanting to make things easier."

Tufty stepped out of the rune chamber, **shivering.** "S-so, it m-makes us more **p-powerful?**"

"Yes. And I would like to see whether it's possible to affect **Chosen Animals.**" Greyfellow's eyes **glowed** more brightly as he glanced at us. "Are any of you willing to serve as my . . . **test subject?**"

Three little paws flew into the air at the same time.

"Me!"

"Me!"

"Me!"

Tufty lumbered toward the chamber again, but Meowz grabbed his tail. "I called it **first!**" she hissed.

He grumbled. "Whatever. Don't **freeze** your tail off, huh?"

With a smirk, **the white nether kitten** zoomed into the rune chamber. "How long do I have to wait in here?"

"**Not too long.**" As the enderman said this, a **gray window** appeared in the air before him. It contained many boxes. In one box was **an image of Meowz.**

He placed a blue cube into one of the boxes. "That's called **lapis lazuli,**" he said. "It's used for this type of thing." The cube disappeared, and a flat image of the cube appeared in the box.

"Almost **done**," he said. "The process should take only a few seconds."

Suddenly, there was **a bright white flash** from inside the chamber. Meowz made the biggest and most terrified-sounding screech before jumping out.

"Mreeeeeeeeeeew! What was that?!"

Greyfellow **smiled**. "That was you being **enchanted**."

"**Really?** I don't feel any different." A screen appeared before her moments later.

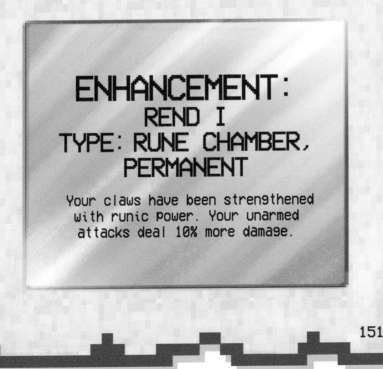

ENHANCEMENT:
REND I
TYPE: RUNE CHAMBER,
PERMANENT

Your claws have been strengthened
with runic power. Your unarmed
attacks deal 10% more damage.

"Look," Tufty said. "**Your claws** are kind of **purple** now."

Meowz held out one of her paws. Indeed, her black claws had **a faint violet glow,** just like the books **Rarg** had dropped earlier.

In addition, **faint little shapes,** almost like weird-looking letters, could be seen upon the surface of her claws. They were also violet, slightly **brighter** than the glow itself.

"This means I can do **more damage?**" she asked.

"**A little,**" Greyfellow said. "**Rend I** isn't very powerful. Sadly, you're not strong enough for anything beyond that."

Greyfellow turned back to the chamber.
"Okay. Who's next?"

(10 minutes later . . .)

Check out
my claws.
(I almost cried.)

So, I've been modified with Rend I.
Every bit helps, right?

It feels kind of **girly** having glowing purple claws, but whatever. I don't care **if my entire body turns bright pink,** so long as it means I no longer have to **run from wolves.**

The rest of the day was spent **training.** After Tufty and Meowz **coughed up** their own ghast fireballs, we **inched silently** across soul sand like **creepers, climbed up** netherrack walls like **spiders, sprinted** like **zombie pigmen,** placed a few items in our inventories, and then

153

swam in that orange fire stuff—err, lava—for over an hour. . . .

There's a huge lake of that stuff in the center of the city. The mobs often go swimming there. They call it a "pool."

And today, that lava pool was filled with hundreds of monsters—a "pool party."

Swimming in lava was so terrifying at first! It took me ten minutes before I could dip one of my paws in. But it didn't burn. Didn't even hurt! Lava is like warm water to me now.

(I still haven't tried drinking it yet. That's on my to-do list.)

By the way, Batwing is immune to lava, too! So, I didn't even need to save him! But he's terrified of swimming . . . Greyfellow actually had to push him in.

Clyde was swimming, too.

Yeah, I haven't told him yet. I keep thinking about how I can say it without hurting his feelings.

I know he'll want to go with me, and I want him to come too, but . . . I don't want him to get hurt. I remember what the sun did to the zombie pigmen and the blazes.

Maybe Clyde could wear a helmet? No, probably not.

Greyfellow could sense how I was feeling. He waded over to me. "Still thinking about your friend, Eeebs?"

"Yes. I'll miss him. I'll miss all of them. I'll even miss you. Thanks for teaching us."

"I'm **glad** I could help," the enderman said. "Listen. Your friend, Clyde. There **is a way** he could go with you."

"**There is?**"

The enderman nodded. "One of the **enhancements** that rune chambers offer is **Sunlight Protection.** Shall we ask him about this?"

"**I suppose,**" I said. "But I want it to be **his** choice."

"**Of course.** Also, I have something you'll need for your return to the Overworld."

"What is it?"

"I'll show you tomorrow. **I think you'll like it.**"

The following morning, I was holding one of those bottle things: a "potion."

"That's a **Potion of Disguise I**," Greyfellow said. "Villager variant. Simply drink it and it will **seem** as though you are an **ordinary** villager."

Clyde stared at the **red liquid** contained within the glass. "Will Eeebs **still be able** to use his abilities?"

"Yes. **Disguise** is merely an **illusion.** Regardless of which form you take, you'll still be able to do everything you could before. Go on, Eeebs. **Don't be afraid. Drink up.**"

"Whatever," I said. "**Here goes.**"

I chugged the potion. The taste . . . yuck! It was like grass mixed with cobblestone. *(Don't ask how I know what those taste like.)*

Thin **white smoke** appeared all around me. To the **gasps** of my friends, I glanced down at myself and found **pale skin** and **brown robes** instead of dark blue fur.

The endermage smirked. "Of course, you'll need to practice standing on **your hind legs** for the illusion to be effective."

"Right."

I tried **standing up** but fell to all fours again.

Meowz began rolling around on the floor: "Ha**haha . . .** that's just . . . **WOW, I** can't. . . ."

Soon, what appeared to be a very real and ordinary villager *(me)* stood before everyone. Although I was **wobbling** around on my feet.

"That potion has a duration of only **one hour**," the endermage said, "so I'll brew **half a stack** for you. Make sure to drink one before going into any town or village. If you must **remain there** for any length of time, drink another before the effects wear off."

"How will I know how much time I have left?" I asked.

"See **that icon** in the lower left corner of your vision?"

"**Got it.** Hey, what about Clyde?"

"**What about me?**" Clyde asked.

"Oh, **man.**" Batwing lowered his head. "You mean, you guys didn't tell him yet?!"

"Well, **um . . .**"

The ghast sniffled. "**Tell me what,** Eeebs?"

"I'm going to the Overworld," I said. "It's part of **my quest.**"

A single tear fell down the ghast's cheek. "**I see.** So, you'll be gone for good?"

"**No way,**" I said. "Come on, Clyde. I'll come back. The Nether is just as much **my home** now as the Overworld is."

"**All right.** Then I guess there's no reason to be sad, right?"

"If you want, you can **come with me.**"

"I can? **How?**"

The enderman then chimed in with how it was possible to **protect** him from sunlight. "It won't make you **immune**," he said, "but you'll be **all right**."

"But it's your choice," I said. "You have to **decide for yourself**."

"Then **I'm staying**," Clyde said. "You know the Overworld, Eeebs. It's best for you to go **alone**. I'll stay here and **help protect** the city in case EnderStar finds us."

Purrrrrrr.

That was **way easier** than I thought.

And Clyde was right. He would be **way more useful** here. "You're sure?" I asked.

"**Definitely.** I know we'll meet again."

And the ghast actually smiled. I mean **actually smiled**. It was like seeing **a flower growing in the Nether**.

I nodded.
"We will."

And so it seemed I was **finally ready**
to venture into **the Overworld.**

With **Rarg's** assistance, the mobs here will try **recruiting** mobs from the nether fortress and work on **defeating** EnderStar.

I want to help with that, of course, but **my destiny** lies elsewhere. Still, Greyfellow **suggested** that it might be possible for the mobs here to join forces with villagers in the Overworld. Together, we could **take out** EnderStar first then deal with **Herobrine** later.

"That really depends on whether anyone in the Overworld is willing to help," Batwing said. "Seems **unlikely.** But then, those villagers **I spoke to** were different from normal villagers."

"**In what way?**" Greyfellow asked.

"Seems like they're **training** to be **warriors.** They know how to wield swords, at least. In fact, they appear to have helped fight off **several large attacks.**"

"**Coordinated** attacks?"

Batwing shrugged. "If your **little crystal** was **accurate,** then yes. The mobs were clearly working together."

"So, **the Eyeless One** has already begun to amass his army."

The endermage nodded. "This is no surprise. We already know that the Prophecy is true. The Great War will soon begin."

"Do you think it's possible that one of those villagers is the one mentioned in that book?" Batwing asked.

"Perhaps. Perhaps that is why you were able to speak with them."

"Why two, though? I thought there was only one Chosen Villager? Well, actually, no. Three. I spoke with a third villager once. What was his name, again? Pebble?"

"I don't have any answer for that," the enderman said. "In fact, there is much I do not know. The tome I have regarding the Prophecy is incomplete. Many pages have been removed."

"One more thing," Batwing said. "Does the Eyeless One know about tellstones?"

"I'm not sure," the endermage said. "Why do you ask?"

"Because that one villager, Pebble, said the Eyeless One was speaking to him in his dreams. Told him that Runt was a spy. A traitor. He appeared in Pebble's dreams at least ten times."

"Why would Herobr—the Eyeless One take such an interest in their village?"

The wither skeleton shrugged. "Beats me. My only guess is he's aware of the Prophecy as well and discovered the identity of the Chosen Villager."

160

"Yes, I suppose you are correct. Hmm."

A villager, two kittens, and a ghast remained silent before Batwing and Greyfellow, trying to understand these mysteries.

Batwing seems to know a lot about what's going on, I thought. And he's always talking to Greyfellow. He must be really important?

As I listened, a realization suddenly hit me. If Batwing is correct, then one of the villagers he spoke with is the same villager I'm supposed to meet.

Breeze. Runt. Pebble. I'm writing these names down here so I don't forget them. I should try to locate them in the Overworld as soon as possible. It's my quest, after all.

"I have a question," I said.

The endermage turned to me. "What is it, Eeebs?"

"Well, you said that I should head to the capital city first. But I'm supposed to meet up with that villager, right? What if he's not in the capital?"

"Hmm. Batwing, do you recall seeing any buildings when using the tellstone?"

"A few times," the skeleton said. "Runt had a nightmare, once. His village had been overrun."

"So, he is in a village, then?"

"I believe so."

"Did you see any buildings made of quartz or clay?"

"None. **Wood** and **cobblestone,** mostly. There was a wall in the distance. Their village was surrounded by **a huge cobblestone wall.**"

"**Interesting.**" The endermage closed his eyes for a moment. "That sounds more like a town, not a village. You're sure they were **villagers?**"

"**Hey,** I'm sure," Batwing said. "Both **Runt** and **Pebble** had **shaved heads** and **huge noses,** while that girl had **super long hair** and a **little nose.** Sound like villagers to you, bud?"

"**Certainly.** I've just never heard of a village **with a wall** before."

"Maybe they're **smarter** than the average villagers?"

"Maybe. **Hmm.**" The enderman closed his eyes again. "**Warriors,** you said. Training to be warriors. Why does that **remind me** of something?"

"Same here," Batwing said. "Wait a second. I thought there was a village in the east like that? **Real serious** folk. Kids start training for combat at the age of **six.**"

"That almost sounds like **Shadowbrook,**" the enderman said. "A village of proud warriors. **Hmm.** Batwing, join me in my library. We have much research to do."

The enderman turned to me. "I'll give you **your answer** soon, Eeebs. For now, rest. Spend time with **your friends.** After today, **you won't have much time for either.**"

After wandering around the streets, I finally found **Rarg.** He was in the center of the city, at the edge of the lava pool, **staring off into space.**

"Hey, Rarg."

"**Hi-lo.** Me friend. Me again want say. **Thank.**"

"No problem. Somehow I just knew you were a **good** guy. I'm glad you **joined us.**"

"Me too. **Boss man crazy.** But **boss man** now-**now** no boss man me. Now-now boss man me **tall gray blink man.** Tall gray blink man no **angry-say** make me black flying **squeaky** thing."

Um . . . What's he talking about?

*Oh. He's saying EnderStar is **no longer his boss.** He now takes orders from the endermage. He doesn't mind, because Greyfellow doesn't* **threaten** *to* **turn him into** *a bat.*

I'm guessing "**angry-say**" *means* **yell?** *And* "**blink**" *must mean* **teleport. . . .**

What's "**now-now,**" *though? Why is it* **repeated?!** *Why do zombie pigmen talk so strangely?!*

"**Yes,**" I said. "**Tall gray blink man** no **angry-say** you. But angry-say me, me no know **breathe fire.** But. Tall gray blink man **happy man.** Most time."

"He **smart** also."

"Yes."

"You. **Name.** Eee . . . bu?"

"**Eeebs,**" I said.

"Eee . . . **buzz.**"

"Close enough."

"**Eeebuzz?** Me want know."

He wants to ask me a question? Hmm, I'm getting better at this.

"You **what** want know?" I asked.

"You go? You go **where-where?**"

"I go **big light.**" I pointed at **the cavernous** ceiling far above. "Big blue. **Yellow square.** You know?"

"Me know. Me no like big blue. Big blue **scare me.** And me eyes hurt me look big yellow square thing. **Eeebuzz?** Me also want know."

"**Yeah?**"

"You. **No feel real?**"

"What you say me **no feel real?**"

"No know. No know. Me no know **how say.**"

"What you say you no know how say? **Me no know.**"

"Me think some time **me no real.** No know how say. But me **no-no feel real.** You?"

He's saying he doesn't feel real? What does he mean by that? Actually, sometimes, I kind of get that feeling. . . . I just assumed it's from all the stress lately?

"Some time," I said. "Yes. Me also no-no feel real."

"Why you me no-no feel real?"

"Me no know."

"Me also no know."

Rarg held up a fish. I'd never seen that kind of fish before. It was dark red in color.

"Me use wood string thing," he said. "Me know how use wood string thing. Wood string thing get red swim-swim. You want eat?"

"Me no want eat. Me eat, you no eat."

"No. Me many red swim-swim."

"Okay."

He handed me the red fish, and I bit into it. It was the best fish I'd ever tasted.

He then pulled another red fish from his inventory and ate it in seconds. He grinned. "Hee hee! You like?"

"It's delicious," I said, taking another bite.

"Delishi . . . ?"

A blank look, until I clarified: "Me think red swim-swim yum-yum."

Wait a second. Where exactly did he get a fish like that?! There's no water in the Nether!

"Rarg. Where you **get** red swim-swim huh?"

He pointed to the lava pool. "There-there. **Orange fire water.**"

Seriously? He caught a fish in the lava?! There's such a thing as lava fish?!

"**How** you get? Can show me **wood string thing** now-now huh?"

"**Okay.**"

He pulled **a strange-looking item** from his inventory. It appeared to be a stick with some **spider string** attached. At the end of the string was something I didn't recognize.

"**You want try?** I try now-now. **You see me try.** Okay?"

"**Okay.**"

For the next hour or so, Rarg showed me **how to fish.** As a cat, we usually just **dived** into the water, but this **wood string thing** made things **way** easier.

Still, using that tool was **difficult** for me at first, as I had to stand up on **my hind legs.** Standing was something I still needed to practice.

And Rarg **wasn't lying.** I eventually caught a **lava fish** of my own, to my complete **surprise.**

I'd originally wanted to find Rarg to see whether maybe Batwing had been right about him being **a spy.** But as we sat down at the edge of the pool, **eating** lava fish in silence, I knew that he was **just as innocent** as me—another **little piece** in what at times felt like some kind of **weird game.**

THURSDAY—UPDATE III

I **curled up** next to my friends on the pink carpeting of the endermage's house.

Still, I couldn't **sleep.** I just kept thinking and thinking and thinking. About the upcoming **war.** About my abilities. About **my quest.** Plus I could hear Greyfellow and Batwing chatting, although I **couldn't make out** what they were saying.

They were in **the secret chamber,** I guess.

At last, I crept over to Greyfellow's **huge bookshelf** and glanced at a few books on the very bottom. This section was labeled **"junk."** When I grabbed several of the books, I quickly understood **why.**

DIARY OF AN ANGRY ENDER EGG

VOLUME 2,152,557

YO, THAT HEROBRINE MAKES ME SO ANGRY. LIKE SO ANGRY. SO TODAY, I SAID TO HIM. "HEROBRINE, U MAKE ME SO ANGRY."

THEN I PLACED A GRASS BLOCK NEARBY. WHY? I DUN KNOW. I JUS DID.

THEN I ATE AN APPLE.

THE END.

WHAT HAPPENS NEXT IN DIARY OF AN ANGRY EGG 2,152,558?!?!
DOES ANGRY EGG EAT A STEAK?

DOES HE?!?!?!

167

DIARY OF A MINECRAFT GRASS BLOCK

Y DOES EVERYONE LIKE PUNCHING ME???

Y DO PPL GRAB ME AND PLACE ME IN WEIRD SPOTS????

Y CANT I JUS GO TO MINECRAFT GRASS BLOCK SCHOOL
AND LEARN HOW TO BE A MINECRAFT GRASS BLOCK LIKE
ALL THE OTHER MINECRAFT GRASS BLOCKS?????

I'm not sure **why,** but I decided to check out *Diary of a Minecraft Grass Block.* There was an introduction, and it read:

There was once a Minecraft grass block named Minecraft Grass Block. Minecraft Grass Block liked doing the things most Minecraft grass block children did. Minecraft Grass Block wanted to learn how to be a better Minecraft grass block, but how would Minecraft Grass Block become a better Minecraft grass block than the other Minecraft grass blocks who hoped to become better Minecraft grass blocks, or at least better Minecraft grass blocks than Minecraft Grass Block was at being a Minecraft grass block and hopefully even the best Minecraft grass blocks a Minecraft grass block could possibly become?

Just turn the page, and follow the adventures of Minecraft Grass Block in this Minecraft Grass Block Diary of a twelve-year-old Minecraft grass block named Minecraft Grass Block, a Minecraft grass block boy who hopes to become a true Minecraft grass block or at least a better Minecraft grass block than the other Minecraft grass blocks.

Wow.
I had no trouble
sleeping afterward.

This morning, I said **my goodbyes.** To Tufty and Meowz. To Clyde, Greyfellow, and Batwing.

Greyfellow gave me more **Disguise potions** and an item called a "compass."

"Remember, you'll want to **keep heading east.**"

Batwing gave me **a tellstone.** "Maybe you'll be able to reach them at some point. **Who knows?**"

Clyde was **crying,** Meowz was about to join him, and Tufty was trying his hardest to be **brave:** "Gonna miss you, man. **Stay safe,** all right?"

"You know me."

"Goodbye, Eeebs," Clyde said. "Thanks for **finding me.**"

"Thanks for **saving my life.**"

"Come back soon, all right?"

"**I will.**"

And that was it. The endermage took me to **the edge of the city,** where he'd built **a nether portal.**

"I will be traveling to the Overworld **as well,**" he said. "Yet, I won't be **joining you.** I'll be traveling to the capital, **Aetheria City.** If you should journey there, ask around for **the Library.** I'll be conducting my research there."

I nodded.

"Now, do you remember **what you must do?**" he asked.

"After I arrive in the Overworld," I said, "I must head **east** and find the village of **Shadowbrook.** It lies on **the east coast** of the main continent. If instead I reach the ocean, I should head **north** until I find it."

"Good. What will you do if you find **this village?**"

"I'll ask to see a girl named **Breeze,**" I said.

"Who else?"

"**Runt. Pebble.**"

"Good. And what will you do if you **cannot locate them?**"

"I'll head **west,** to **Aetheria City,** and find you."

"And if you do come across them?"

"I will tell them they need to **abandon their village,**" I said, "and seek refuge in the capital."

"Why?"

I **crept** forward, trying to recall what he'd told me earlier. "Because according to **the Prophecy, a dragon** is going to burn it to the ground."

"**Excellent.** It seems your **Higher Intelligence** ability really does work."

". . ."

I remembered **the first time** I'd stepped into a nether portal. The **uncertainty** I'd felt, then. **The fear.** The hesitation.

Now, it was much like that, only **ten times worse**. I was **afraid** of what I'd see and what I might have to face. At last, I stepped in.

My vision **wavered**.
All grew dark.

As soon as I arrived in the Overworld, I began **sprinting.**

At first, everything looked **normal.** Trees. Tall grass. Hills and mountains, rivers and valleys.

But I soon came across the kind of things I'd hoped I wouldn't see. . . .

As common as the holes left from explosions were the charred remains of many trees.

Within hours,
I found a village—
or what looked like one to me. . . .

Yet blasted crops and scattered rubble were all that I could see.

There were no sounds here beyond the low whistle of the wind.

Even the farm animals had disappeared.

I **sniffed** around every building.

*Not picking up any **villager scent**,* I thought. *Whatever happened here must have happened **days** or even **weeks** ago.*

Yet, within minutes, I caught **two new scents.** One was **human,** the other **villager.** I soon heard them **approaching** so I hid in some tall grass nearby.

(My Creep ability must have turned me mostly invisible, as they didn't seem to notice me.)

The human had spiked **yellow hair** and brown armor, and he carried **a sword** on his back. The villager had a huge nose and carried **two swords** on his back, one sword slightly smaller than the other.

"I can't **believe** this," the villager said. "It's **just** like the last one I saw."

"**Get used to it,**" the human said. "Every place I've come across has been like this. **Or worse.**"

The villager suddenly seemed **so angry.** His rage quickly subsided, however, and he gazed at the ruins in **sorrow.**

"**C'mon,**" the human said. "Let's look around and see if there's anything we can **salvage.** And stay alert. You wouldn't believe the stuff that's out here."

"I'd believe. I've **fought** a few myself."

"**Really?** Hey. Why are you out here, anyway?"

"**I was exiled.**"

"What'd you do?"

"I made **a wrong decision.** . . . . It's a long story."

"They at least gave you **a weapon** or something, right? Some **tools?**"

"**None.** I'd dropped all my stuff earlier. That first night, I was jumped by **ten husks** while trying to dig **an emergency shelter.**"

"**Ouch.** Did you even have a sword at that point?"

"No. Just **a wooden shovel.**"

"You fought **ten husks** with a wooden shovel? How'd you manage **that?**"

"I just managed." The villager **paused.** "Why are **you** out here?"

"**Because of this.**" The human withdrew **a piece of paper** from his inventory. "Found it in some **ruins** a few days ago. In a library. It leads to **a cave filled with adamant.**"

"What's **adamant?**"

The human sighed. "I think you've been **holed up** in that village of yours for way too long. Maybe getting **exiled** wasn't such a bad thing, **huh?** Anyway, I'll show you the ropes. Just **stick with me.**" He **drew** his sword.

176

"C'mon. That cave isn't too far from here. We'll **search this place** first then hit the cave afterward."

"All right," the villager said. "By the way, you never told me **your name.**"

"**Just call me S,**" the human said.

"**S? That's it?**"

"Well, I know my name **starts** with an S. I can't seem to remember the rest, though. Anyway, **let's go.**"

They took off.

Of course, I wanted to **reveal** myself and speak with them, but they looked **a little dangerous.**

Once they were **far enough** away, I took out my compass and left the ruins, heading east again. For the rest of the day, the only thing I found of interest was fire. **A forest fire.**

In my dreams, I heard voices.
The voices of two girls.

"Dude. Scouting is totally lame. Nothing has happened for days!"

"It's what we've been tasked with, Emerald. It's for the safety of our village."

"Yeah. I know. I just miss hot baths, y'know? I'm totally caked in grime, these new boots are hurting my feet, and—hey, look! Over there!"

"Is that an ocelot?"

"Looks like it. What's up with the blur fur, though?"

"What were you saying about nothing interesting happening?"

"I stand corrected. This is even more interesting than that human girl showing up at our village. What's her name again?"

"ilovedragons1. Why do some of the humans have such odd names?"

"Who knows. Hey, why isn't this ocelot waking up?!"

Finally, as I felt something nudge me, **my eyes flew open.**

"He's adorable!" the girl with greenish-blue hair exclaimed.

"Is that even an ocelot?" the other girl asked. *"Looks more like a monster to me."*

"Whatever he is, I say we keep him."

178

"Keep him?! **Are you joking?!** I thought you didn't like monsters, **Breeze.**"

"Wouldn't a monster be **attacking** us by now?"

"Yeah, I guess."

"It's **strange,** though. I thought ocelots were **afraid** of people? Has he already been **tamed?**" It took a moment for the **realization** to hit.

Breeze?! The girl on the left is **Breeze?!** Is that some kind of luck or what?!

I rose to all fours and **yawned.** "You don't need to talk as if I **can't understand you.** I'm well versed in **your language.**"

The girls **jumped back.** "**Um,** like, did he just . . ."

"**You can really talk?**" Breeze asked.

"Yeah?"

"Why do I feel things are about to get **crazy** around here again?" Emerald said.

"I've been sent to find **a girl named Breeze**," I said. "Also, **two boys.** One goes by the name of **Runt.** The other is known as **Pebble.**"

The girls exchanged glances.

"I don't understand," Breeze said. "How do you **know about us?**"

"Through our mutual friend. **Batwing.**"

Her smile **faded.**

Emerald **sighed.** "Um, is he talking about that skeleton you've been **dreaming about?**"

"Yes."

"Right. Shall we head back now and warn the mayor of **impending craziness** the likes of which we've never seen?"

Breeze **slowly nodded** at her, before staring into my eyes. "What's your name?"

"**Eeebs.**"

"**Nice to meet you,** Eeebs. May I ask why you were sent to find us?"

"It's **a long story.**"

"**That's fine.** Would you like to head back to our village with us? You can tell us on the way."

"**Of course,**" I said. "Oh, and now that you mention it, I should say that I've been instructed to **inform you** of something. Regarding your village."

The girls exchanged glances again. "What is it?" Breeze asked.

"All of you should leave **before the moon is full,**" I said, "and head to **the capital,** as according to **the Prophecy** . . . your village is about to be <u>**annihilated**</u>."

SUNDAY—UPDATE I

While searching for the village of **Shadowbrook,** I met **two girls** named **Emerald** and **Breeze.**

I told them about how I was sent to **find them** and how, according to **the Prophecy,** their village would soon be **destroyed.**

Come to find out, I was **never** going to find **Shadowbrook.** It was Breeze's **home village,** and it was completely **wiped out** some time ago. She's one of the **survivors** who fled.

"**Wait,**" I said. "Where are you taking me, then?"

"**Villagetown.** We believe it's the last village still standing on this side of the continent."

"Well, **the humans** say it's not really **a village,**" Emerald said, "but **a town.** And maybe they're right, y'know? It's changed so much."

"**It has.**" Breeze turned away. We were standing on a large hill overlooking a river, and she pointed at something far away. I'd never seen **anything like it** before.

"Is that some kind of tree?" I asked.

Breeze **shook her head.** "It's one of our **watchtowers.** It also functions as a **beacon.** Our builders constructed them around our village to help the **scouts** find their way back."

182

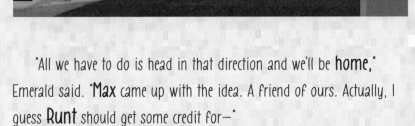

"All we have to do is head in that direction and we'll be **home**," Emerald said. "**Max** came up with the idea. A friend of ours. Actually, I guess **Runt** should get some credit for—"

I almost **jumped** when she said his name. "**You know Runt?!**"

"**Of course,**" Emerald said. "He's part of our **group.** In fact, he **should** be with us right now."

"Why isn't he?"

"He's currently being **punished.**" To my **blank expression,** Emerald sighed. "We recently graduated from school, and the mayor gave us **one last** little school assignment. We had to write **twenty pages** about our chosen profession. Now, I love my village and all, and I have absolutely **zero regrets** about becoming a **warrior,** but dude

. . . c'mon. Who wants to write twenty pages about **anything?** Luckily, **Runt** thought of a way for us to avoid writing so much without **breaking the rules,** and every other student **copied Runt's idea.** Needless to say, the mayor wasn't too **thrilled** about that. Guess that's why **Runt** is back to crafting **potato-based food items.**"

Resisting the urge to ask, *"What's a potato?"* I **nodded.** "Hmm. Do you think I'll be able to speak with him?"

"Probably," Emerald said. "That is, if the entire village doesn't freak out upon hearing the bad news. By the way, what kind of **dragon** is supposed to attack?"

"I have no idea. **I don't even know what a dragon is.**"

". . ."

After the girls took me to their **village,** I was **surrounded** by so many people. No one seemed to be **afraid** of me—not even the children:

"Is that really **an ocelot?**"

"It looks more like **a monster!**"

"**Wow!** Where can I get one of those?!"

I've never been picked up before. Or petted. Or hugged. Or given so much food.

I can get used to this. I **love** Villagetown.

"Thanks for **the fish**," I said, to a human boy named **LazyGiraffe.** "An hour of sprinting can really drain your food bar."

"You can **talk?!**"
"Hey, what's **your name?!**"
"What kind of ocelot **are you,** huh?!"

My introduction to **Villagetown** went pretty much like that.

A girl named **Ophelia** gave Breeze a hug. **"Glad to see you back safely.** What's the deal with this guy?"

"It's **complicated,**" Breeze said.

Emerald laughed. "I'll say. Just wait until you hear **the news.**" She turned to Ophelia. **"Hey.** Your dad's a **librarian,** right? Ever heard about something called **the Prophecy?**"

"I haven't. Why?"

"Never mind." Emerald glanced farther into the village. **"I'm out.** Time for a bath. See you guys at **the meeting?**"

Ophelia blinked. **"What meeting?**"

But Emerald only winked before taking off.

"Um, **okay?**" The yellow-haired girl turned to Breeze. "What's going on?"

"Seems like this kitten came from **a city of monsters,**" Breeze said. **"Good ones.**" She reached down and **scratched my neck.** "Isn't that right?"

"I don't **consider** myself to be a monster," I said, **"but yes.** You are correct."

186

"So, why are you here?" Ophelia asked me.

"Have you ever heard of someone known as a Savior?"

"No?"

"How about Chosen Ones?"

"Um . . ."

The other villagers looked just as confused.

Moments later, a man known as the mayor approached, along with many serious-looking men in black clothes.

"Breeze? What's going on here?! And . . . what is that?!"

"We found him sleeping under a tree. He has a message for us."

"Right." The mayor stared at me without blinking for at least five seconds. "Um. Good work."

One of the men in black robes threw something around my neck—I'd later come to learn that it was a leash.

I hissed and tried running away, but whenever I moved more than five blocks away from my captor, I flew back toward him.

Breeze moved up to the man. "Father, stop!"

He smiled slightly. His eyes were concealed by these weird-looking black things. "You know what must be done."

SUNDAY—UPDATE III

They **hauled me** away to a small, dark room and asked countless questions. The kind of questions **cautious people** ask when **a blue kitten** suddenly shows up at their village.

"Did Herobrine send you?!"

"Good monsters?! In the Nether?!"

Yes, it's true. And their breath isn't nearly as stinky as yours.

I told them **everything,** but they **didn't believe** a word. No one had heard of **the Prophecy,** and as for **dragons . . .**

"The Overworld hasn't seen **dragons** for over **a thousand years!**" the man named **Brio** shouted. "**One kind of dragon** still lives on, yes, but only in the **third dimension!**"

"All I know is what I've been told! The enderman gave me this book, and . . ."

After I talked about the book Greyfellow had loaned me, Brio brought in more villagers. They wore white robes.

I came to learn that they were librarians and had in-depth knowledge of this world's history. Yet, none of them could recall ever reading about the Prophecy.

"What about these abilities you speak of?" the mayor asked. "Care to demonstrate them?"

"Sure."

To their awe, I breathed fire, climbed a nearby cobblestone wall, and turned almost invisible when standing still.

"If there was a pool of lava nearby," I said, "I could go for a swim. I'm immune to fire, just like the monsters that live in the Nether."

Finally, I summoned my visual enchantment screen. Brio and the mayor recognized it immediately. Amazingly, they had visual enchantments as well. They summoned them using their mind, the same as I had.

"Almost every living being has them," Brio said. "Yet, most are unable to access them. They must be . . . unlocked."

The two villagers closed their screens, and the mayor looked at mine, which was currently displaying my enhancements. "What's that?"

"The enderman **enchanted me** somehow," I said, and held up **my purple claws.**

"Did he ask you to step into **a metallic box** of some kind?" Brio asked.

"You mean **a rune chamber?**"

"Yes." Brio turned to the mayor. "Perhaps **he speaks the truth?**"

The mayor nodded. "Listen . . . **Eeebs,** is it? I'm going to call everyone in the village. We're going to have **a meeting.**"

"You'll need to tell **everyone** what you've told us just now," Brio added. For **some reason,** he was smiling again in that strange way. "I suppose we'll soon be making **yet another alliance.**"

The man named **Drill** spoke up. "Tell me **this creature** is joining our army. Please. I want this thing **on the front lines.**"

"Perhaps he will." Brio stopped smiling. "One last thing, **kitten.** Did that book mention the names of the **two Saviors?**"

"Yes. But I **forgot** them. The enderman asked me to remember so many different things. The book said that one of them was a **human.** Does that help?"

"Not exactly."

An hour later, I stood in a **fancy-looking area** of Villagetown. A countless number of villagers had **gathered** before me.

Wait, no. Roughly half of them **weren't** villagers. They looked **different** . . . wore different **clothes.** Perhaps they were **the humans** I'd heard about?

(Now that I think about it, I've seen villagers several times before, back when I was just a normal kitten, but I don't recall ever seeing humans until today. Where'd they come from?)

The mayor eventually **introduced me** and asked me to tell everyone the news.

By "help save the world," the Prophecy actually meant "serve as a messenger."

I suppose it **was strange** for them to hear an animal speak.

Stranger still to hear me speak of **a city** filled with **monsters** willing to cooperate.

"The monsters I met know about **magic**," I said. "They're **very smart**. I believe both sides could **help each other**."

Of course, there were many who didn't believe or **trust** me. Such as a young man who **emerged** from the crowd. A human, I think? He **looked up** at the mayor and called out:

"Sir? Do you think it's **a good idea** to work with monsters?"

When I saw him, I could **sense** that there was something **different** about him. It was the **same feeling** I got after meeting **Greyfellow, Batwing, Brio, Breeze, Emerald. . . .**

Still, he was **different** from even them. **Stronger,** maybe? Was the **power** I sensed due to him being higher in level and possessing stronger abilities than the rest? **I'm not sure.**

"You certainly have a point," the mayor said to this human. "We will **discuss** this at length and have a vote."

This caused a **huge commotion.** The crowd only grew louder when the mayor added: "Although it's **hard to imagine,** there may come a time when **monsters live among us** an—"

An old villager man **glared** at me and shouted, "The day I live alongside monsters is the day I **make my own village! I know how to dig!** I'll make an underground house and start a bat farm!"

More villagers joined in:

"I'm with you, **Leaf!**"

"**Me too!** This is madness!"

"No one's even heard of this **Prophecy!**"

"If **a dragon** really does attack, we'll be ready! We've already fended off **thousands of zombies!**"

"Working **with** monsters?! How can anyone **suggest** such a thing?! Do you not remember the attacks?!"

"**No mobs allowed!**" someone screamed.

"Yeah! **No mobs allowed!**"

Roughly half of the crowd began **chanting** this phrase. Then someone **threw a carrot at me.** This was followed by some **seeds,** an apple, and, finally, a loaf of bread.

(I ate the bread, topping off my food bar, so the joke was on them.)

"**Stop this at once!**" the mayor shouted. "We cannot **ignore** what this animal has to say! If there really are **good** monsters out there, we must consider forming **an alliance!**"

He left the raised platform and stood **next to me.** "Even though

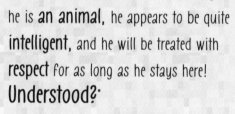

he is **an animal,** he appears to be quite **intelligent,** and he will be treated with **respect** for as long as he stays here! **Understood?**"

There were many **grumbles,** weak attempts at protest. But just as many people walked up to me. **Including Breeze.**

"I'd like to **take him around** and teach him more about our village," she said to the mayor. "**Is that okay?**"

No, that's not a redstone generator. That's me. Purring.

"Only if Eeebs agrees to it." He sighed. "Kitten, I'm sorry for their outburst. We're a little distrustful of monsters. That being said, do you really wish to stay here for the time being?"

"Why not? I like being held."

"Very well. In the meantime, our librarians will do more research. We'll see if we can shed some light upon this mysterious Prophecy you speak of. And you'll be able to speak with Runt after he's . . . through with his punishment."

"Thank you." I suddenly remembered the human's words. "Sir."

"I'm exhausted," Breeze said to her father. "I'll take him back to our house and show him Villagetown tomorrow."

As she turned around, holding me in her arms, she bumped into another person. A villager in a dark red robe. A bunch of white hair hung from the lower part of his face, and he was wearing a huge red hat and the same black things Breeze's father wore. You couldn't see much of his face.

"Sorry," he said. "**Forgive me,** my lady."

She stepped closer to him. "**Hey,** don't I know you?"

"**N-no,** no. I . . . no, I don't believe we've met before. Yes, certainly I'd remember a **damsel** such as yourself!"

"What's your name?"

"**My name?**" He paused. "**Korbius!**" He nodded **profusely.** "Yes, that's my name! **Korbius Wijjibo!**"

"I don't recall ever seeing you in Villagetown before."

"Of course not, for I am . . . **a traveling merchant!** Yes! A merchant who travels! That's **meeee!**" He bowed. "Would you like to trade?"

"No thanks." Breeze lingered in front of him for a moment, **her brow furrowed,** then carried me off. It was **strange,** the way she acted.

"What's wrong?" I asked, still purring.

"**Nothing.**" She glanced back at him. "**Guess I'm just paranoid.**"

When we entered Breeze's house, I was **shocked** at how **small** it seemed. Compared to Greyfellow's hut, it was **tiny.** Her bedroom was **five blocks wide.**

> Emerald said earlier that Breeze's room almost looks like a dungeon. I kinda have to agree.

I **sat down** on the carpet. "Is it really **so hard to believe** that **good monsters** exist?"

"We've been through a lot," she said. "**Monsters attacked** several times already, and some of us were . . . well . . . **we've lost people.**"

"**I'm sorry.** Then I guess I can understand why they're so **distrustful.**"

I **sniffed around** and saw a book lying on top of a raised flat surface. It was **a diary,** just like mine.

Dear Diary,
I miss him.

*Where did she learn how to **draw** like that? I'm so **jealous.***

She **rushed over** and **closed the diary** before I had a chance to really look at the drawing. Her cheeks were **so red!**

"That's **Runt,** right?"

"Yes. You've . . . seen him before, haven't you?"

"Yeah. **Using one of these.**" I withdrew the **tellstone** from my inventory and told her about it.

"That **explains** a lot," she said. "I was beginning to think **Herobrine** was behind those dreams. Maybe we could **use this** tonight to speak with Runt?"

"Maybe. Batwing said his tellstone didn't always work, though. Tellstones should be able to **communicate** with anyone, sleeping or not. But they're **hard to craft.** The enderman is still working on **perfecting** them."

"Well, if it doesn't work, you can always speak to Runt in person. He'll be **free** in a few days."

"Do they **always** punish him like that?"

"**No,** it's just . . . he's a **captain,** now. **A leader.** Kind of. So the mayor wants him to set **a good example.** A lot of the younger kids **look up to him** now."

"Oh."

Later that night, we **tried using** the tellstone.

I pictured **Runt** in my mind, but nothing appeared. Then, for some reason, I thought of that villager I'd seen yesterday. **The crystal immediately lit up:**

The images **disappeared**. The **purple gleam** returned to the crystal's surface. I pawed the tellstone every which way, but **the images wouldn't return.**

(I'm not positive on this, but I believe he was having a **nightmare** and woke up, which **severed** the tellstone's connection.)

"That was **Pebble,**" Breeze said. "So . . . did we just witness **his dreams** or something?"

"I think so."

200

"Didn't think he was **still alive.**"

"He is," I said. "I saw him yesterday. Before I met you."

"**Where?**"

"In some **ruins.** He was with a human. They were searching around for **a cave.**"

"So, he really did survive. . . ." She said something after this, but **so quietly,** as if speaking to herself. "He must have learned how to use **abilities,** too."

Well, **I think** that's what she said.
Or did I just **imagine** her saying that?

Breeze gave me a **tour** of the village today.

While we walked through the streets, I noticed these **large pieces of paper** called **"posters."** They were everywhere. Someone must have put them up **last night.**

NO MOBS
ALLOWED!

"Seems like at least a few people haven't forgotten **the meeting**," I said.

"It was **hard enough** getting everyone to agree to let **humans** stay here. I'm not so sure we'll ever be able to form **an alliance** with monsters."

"Well, we've got to **try.** They're really **so nice. You'd like them.**"

We soon forgot about the posters, because **a villager in white robes** ran up to us.

Max. He's a **warrior** like Breeze, but he once had interest in becoming a **librarian.**

"I've read **nearly every book** in the village," he said, "and found nothing relating to **the Prophecy.** However . . ."

He held up a book *(History of Minecraftia, Volume II)* and turned to somewhere in the middle. "**Look.** Someone **tore out** three pages."

Breeze ran her fingers across the jagged edges. "**Why would they do that?**"

Max shrugged. "Maybe it said something about **the Prophecy?** But who would want to **hide** that? **The mayor?**"

"No, I don't think so," Breeze said. "Wait. Where did you get this book?"

"The main library. I'll go there again tomorrow and double-check for any other books that might have been tampered with. Wanna join me?"

"Sorry. Today's my only day off this week, and I'm supposed to show Eeebs around."

"It's cool. Emerald's off tomorrow. I'll ask her." He glanced at me. "Really wish you could've brought that book you were talking about."

"I could always go back for it," I said.

"You might have to," Max said, "if nothing turns up."

Max then took off, and Breeze showed me so many different places.

The villagers have this food called "ice cream." Some of it was crafted to look like a creeper's head. Why would they do that? I really don't understand.

It almost felt like someone was watching us. But I didn't see anyone. . . .
One street had something really weird. A villager did something known as
a "farming fail."

Hours later, as Breeze explained **the combat cave** to me, that **Drill**
guy ran up to us.

He **screamed** so loudly, asking Breeze if she was done accompanying
"His Royal Fuzziness" around. Was he talking about me?!

"You want a little tour of our village, huh?" He pointed down a street.
"See all those people **building** and farming!? That's called **hard work!**
You'll be **joining them** if you wanna stay here! **Now march!**"

Drill thinks I need to be **trained.** Long story short, I've been asked to **help out.** If I want to stay here, I must become **a useful member** of the village.

They seem to think I'd make **a great scout.** That means exploring beyond the wall. But scouts should know all the **basics,** such as **mining, crafting,** and **farming. . . . It's dangerous,** being a scout. They say the monsters outside are growing stronger. It's an **important** job, too, because scouts are supposed to search for **resources** like iron.

It seems that **iron** is **really important** to these villagers. They use it to make weapons, armor, tools, and even defenses such as doors and gates. The **problem** is that iron comes from the ground, and they've **already mined** most of the ground beneath the village. They say they don't want to go any deeper because it's **too dangerous.**

Food is also a concern. A large number of humans arrived some time ago. The farms here can produce **only so much food.** Right now, people are **consuming more** than can be grown. So they need to make more farms. They've used up almost all the land within the walls, though, which means they must start farming **outside.**

As we followed **Drill** through the streets, he kept yelling at random villagers, telling them to build **faster,** work **harder:**

"You're **lollygagging** like **Stump** in a kitchen! Like **Runt** at the ice cream stand! Like **Emerald** in the Clothing Castle!" In a **much calmer** voice, he said, "In fact, I bet that's where I'll find her. Come on, kitten. Let's go say hello to **your new teacher.**"

I saw **Brio** and **the mayor** at one point. They were **yelling** at workers as well. The word **"efficiency"** was often brought up.

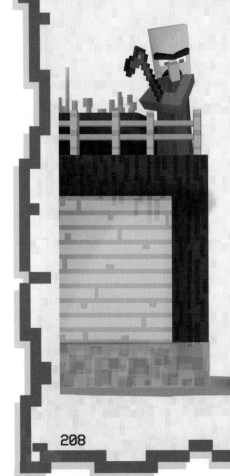

"Build farms on the houses!"

"Don't waste any space!"

Efficient use of space. Proper building techniques. What are they talking about?! I don't even know what a crop is!

Later on, Drill took us to this place called **the Clothing Castle.** Apparently, Emerald really does spend **a lot of time** there.

"Hey, guys! Wanna go shopping with me?"

"Err, I meant trading. I totally wasn't trying to sound like a human. Yeah."

"How did I know I'd find you **here?**" Drill said.

Emerald glanced sideways to the left and right **without moving her head. "Oh!** Are you talking **to me?** Need some **fashion advice,** huh?"

"Hardly. Since Breeze will be **scouting** tomorrow, and since **you're off** tomorrow, you'll be the first one to teach this kitten. **Help him get up to speed.** Show him how to **farm.**"

"**What?** But I was supposed to go fishing and—"

"What's that? You said you're ready to do **five thousand laps** around the combat yard?"

She flashed a smile. A **nervous** one. "Did I say **fishing?!** It's been a long day! What I meant was I'd be **honored** to teach Eeebs! **Where should I begin?**"

Emerald taught me **how to farm** today.

I personally think it went **very well,** but she seems to think **otherwise.**

Hey, it's not **my fault.** Her instructions weren't very **clear** to me. As if **a kitten** would know anything about **planting seeds!**

Place them on the ground, she said.

That's all I need to do, she said.

"Dude! Don't be in **such a rush!** You need to place seeds in **farmland!**"

She took me to **a grassy area** where she demonstrated how to use this farming tool called a **"hoe."**

Standing on my hind legs again, I **turned three blocks of grass into farmland** and planted some seeds. I felt **so proud** of myself. She didn't, though.

"Farmland should be **close together**," she said. "There's no need to have it all **scattered around** like that."

"Right."

"Okay. I finally got it figured out. Can I go now?"

"Dude? Where's the **water?** You really need to **listen!**"

She told me again about how crops need to be **watered,** or **irrigated.** Otherwise, they won't grow nearly as fast.

I did pretty well, **all things considered.** She gave me a bucket, and I **scooped up some water.** I just forgot about the **"digging a hole for the water"** part.

A minor setback, **nothing more!**

"Hey! I didn't say dump the water on top!"

"Well, at least the farmland is irrigated now!"

Okay, I've got the water placed correctly.

There's no way I can mess anything up from here.

"What?!?! How am I supposed to know the difference between a flower and a potato?!"

"I've seen a lot of farming fails, but **wow. Just wow.**"

"Isn't diversity a good thing, though?"

All right, I've got this farming stuff figured out. BRB, time to ace the rest and become the ultimate farming champion.

She said I needed to protect my crops. So I did. Not even sunlight will get to them.

"**Come on!** Crops need **light** to grow! You can't just build **a wall** around them!"

"Okay! **Okay!** I'm sorry! I just want to talk to **Runt,** okay? It's part of **my quest!** I can't stop thinking about it!"

"Yeah? Do you have **any idea** what they'll make us do if they catch us sneaking up to him? You'll see **Runt** when he's no longer crafting **baked potatoes**, okay? **Just follow the rules!**"

"Fine!"

Using **a pickaxe,** I began tearing down the wall.

"**Good kitten.** Now, what you should do is build a **fence.** Here, I'll place the crafting table again and . . ."

So I need a fence instead of a cobblestone wall. From here, absolutely nothing else can go wrong. I'm certain of it.

For the first time today, Emerald **smiled.** "Good job."

"How about **a hug,** huh? Or you can just **scratch my chin.** I'm not picky."

"I'll pet you once we're finished. Now listen up. Okay, so, crops need light, **right?** But what happens when the sun goes down? How can you provide light for your crops during the night? **Any ideas?**"

"I **think** so."

According to what she said, with this much light, the crops will grow **ultra fast!**

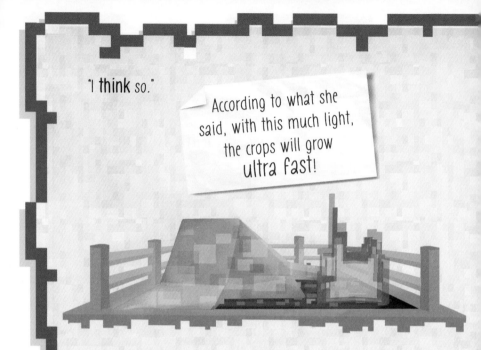

Emerald **facepalmed.** "We're done for the day. And tomorrow, **Stump** will be teaching you **how to craft,** not me."

"Okay. By the way, **where's my hug?**"

"As if! **Hurmmph!**"

Emerald **stormed off.** Later, a nice girl named **Lola** taught me how to shoot this weapon called a **"bow."**

The other villagers say she used to be very unskilled, but she's recently **shown promise.** She also crafted **a hat** out of a **creeper** she dropped in the wild.

"Told you I'd get better!"

Nessa "Lola" Diamondcube
from Noob Extraordinaire to Scout First Class.

EXPLORER'S CAP

ARMOR (+2.5)

+ 5% VIEW DISTANCE
+ 10% STEALTH BONUS
+ 3% ACCURACY WITH BOWS
+ 15% CRITICAL DAMAGE BONUS
+ 25% MAP DRAWING ACCURACY

This morning, I met the villager known as **Stump**. One of Runt's **best friends.**

He wasn't **too happy** about having to teach me on his **day off.** Part of the problem was that I kept eating **the crafting ingredients.**

He called me a **walking garbage can,** because according to him, it's not even possible to **eat** some of those ingredients. Our time together can be summarized by **a single picture:**

"Craft something!!"

Notice my blank stare.

(I'd include pictures of my various crafting fails, but at this point, I've become somewhat embarrassed of my complete lack of skill.)

I guess Stump takes his crafting **seriously**—especially **food items** like cakes—so when I basically **decorated** the floor with ingredients, his anger only grew.

Luckily, **Max** interrupted us before long. He just burst through the door, **muttering something** about books and libraries and **the biggest mystery** the village has ever seen.

Seconds later,
we were out the door.

Max took us to one of Villagetown's **libraries**—the **biggest one** in the village.

"I've been doing **a lot of research** here," he said, leading us past the bookshelves. "I found a book with missing pages in one of the back rooms. . . . But I didn't notice **the carpet** until this morning," he said.

Stump glanced around. **"What's wrong with it?** Besides that **awful** orange color, I mean. **Seriously,** who decorated this place?"

Max walked farther into the room, then stopped. **"Come over here."**

We followed. As an animal who'd only **just** learned how to farm, I had **no idea** what was going on. But then, I didn't feel too bad, because Stump didn't seem to understand either.

Max pointed at the floor.

Carpeting made from a **sheep's wool** and dyed bright orange.

That should have been nothing more than a decoration, something placed over cobblestone.

"Feels a little **soft**," Stump said, stepping on to one section of the carpet. "**Spongey,** really. Almost like a cake. **What, is there nothing underneath?**"

Max **mined** the carpet up with his bare hands.

He'd discovered a secret.

Max thinks it's been here for **a very long time.**

The ladder led to a secret little chamber.

What sat inside were more bookcases, a chest filled with all kinds of papers and scrolls . . . and **a massive tome,** lying on a table.

Although it looked like nothing more than a large book with a **dark gray cover,** there was **something** about it—the more I stared, the more I sensed **the power** it contained.

Max lifted the tome up in a way that suggested an **immense weight.** *Record of Aetheria* was its name. "It just goes on and on. It's over **five hundred pages** long."

"Five hundred pages?!" Stump moved closer and eyed it suspiciously. "Of what?"

"The history of the world. **The Prophecy,** too. And guess who's name is in here?"

"Breeze?"

"No. **Kolb.**"

I zoomed over to take a better look at the tome. "He's **one of the Saviors,** right?"

"Apparently. I'm wondering why he **never told us?**"

"Maybe he doesn't know?" Stump said.

Max shrugged. "It gets **weirder.** One of the things I've read . . . we're supposedly controlled by some kind of **guiding force** called **AI.**"

"I've heard that before," I said.

Max turned to the first page. "There's also this."

DO NOT LET HIM SEE

HE FEARS THEM

BUT HE DOES NOT KNOW WHO THEY ARE

EYELESS ONE ALWAYS WATCHING

HIDE

ALWAYS BEHIND YOU

HE WAITS

"Whoever wrote this **clearly** didn't want **Herobrine** reading it," Stump said. "That must be why it was **stashed** here. But who wrote it?"

Max turned to the next page.

RECORD OF AETHERIA

ORIGINALLY WRITTEN BY ENTITY303

EDITED BY THE FIVE SCRIBES:
MANGO, IMPULSE75, DIAMOND GIRL,
SPARKLE, PHRED13

"We have to ask **Kolb** about this," Stump said. "**He has to know something.**"

Max nodded. "I'll go see if I can find him. You two wait here. **And Eeebs?** Wipe that sugar off your nose. Seriously, man. **Are you a kitten or a pig?**"

Ten or so minutes later, **Kolb** entered the cramped little room.

"There'd better be **a good reason** for bringing me down here," he said. "**I really—**" He paused when he saw me. "**Oh.** So it's about that. How many have you told, **kitten?**"

"**No one.** I couldn't remember your name."

"So you already **know?**" Max asked.

"**Yeah.**"

"Can you please just tell us what's going on?" Stump asked.

The human sat down on a bookcase. "I can tell you what I know. Of course, **for the safety of your village,** you must **promise never** to tell anyone else. Not even the mayor. **Agreed?**"

Two villagers and a kitten nodded their heads in unison.

Kolb **sighed.** "You know, I used to **laugh at myself** for talking with what I once considered to be NPCs. But now . . . **whatever.** Here it goes."

And so, **he told us his story.**

The human named Kolb once lived in a world known as **Earth.**

His life was **fairly boring** back then. He went to school, did homework, studied. He also **played games.**

The games he played utilized a **technology** known as **virtual reality.** You threw on a **helmet-like** device, and it seemed like you were in **another world.**

His mom was always working, and he'd **never known** his father, so he often escaped into games to not feel so alone. His favorite place was a virtual reality **Minecraft server** called **Aetheria.**

That world is **this world.** Or used to be.

Max didn't seem to believe him. "You're telling me . . . we're just **game** characters?"

"I don't know," Kolb said. "We still don't know for sure. We've had countless arguments over this, trying to figure it all out."

"Well, what happened?" Stump asked. "You said this game you played was **normal,** right? **Everyone** played it. So **what changed?** Why are all the humans always **freaking out?**"

"**Umm** . . . it's like this. . . ."

The human then shared more of his story.

It was the year **2039,** and his world was in a similar situation as our own: suffering from **a terrible war.** One day, weapons capable of **unparalleled destruction** were sent through the air, toward his homeland. When this was announced, he was **alone.**

In the eyes of many, **the world was about to end.** So Kolb, wanting to at least see his friends one last time, **entered the virtual reality world of Aetheria.** To say **goodbye.**

There, he met his **best friend, Ione,** as well as one of the game's administrators, **Entity.**

However . . .

With **the world's destruction** just minutes away . . .

"I **blacked out** and woke up still in the game," he said, "**unable** to log out. We call it **the event.** Many of us think there's a **scientific** explanation for what happened. Yet, just as many believe in the **impossible.**"

Max looked up from **the massive tome.** "You mean **magic?**"

"Yeah. I guess so. I've never believed in **that kind of stuff.** Still don't. Yet . . . some humans think Entity is a wizard who whisked them away to safety just before the world ended."

"So that's why you guys have those **arguments,**" Stump said. "Some of you call yourselves **Believers,** and others are **Seekers.** I never understood why until now."

"If we really are **game characters,**" Max said, "does that mean we're **not really alive?** We're just like . . . **golems,** or something? Following **instructions** of some kind?"

The human shrugged. "We've spent days discussing that. In the end, each of you seems **very real**, so . . . it really is like the game **magically** came to life." He sighed. "**Look,** guys. I'm just telling you what I know, and what I know isn't much. It took me a long time to **come to terms** with this. But I've finally accepted it. **It is what it is.**"

"I don't meant to interrupt," I said, "but **I'm starving.** Maybe we could talk more over dinner?"

The other three looked at me as if I'd just asked if they wanted to help **build a snow fort** in the Nether.

"It's not even **lunchtime,**" Max said.

"**Oh.** What can I say? I've been living in the Nether. Having no sky kinda messes with your **sense of time.**"

Stump retrieved a **strange-looking** item from his inventory and placed it on to one of the bookcases. It had a **familiar** scent. . . .

"Here. Eat this and be quiet. It's delicious. Promise."

"Is that a work of masterful crafting or some kind of giant mutated mushroom?"

—Max

I sniffed again. "What is **that?!**"

"**A stormberry cake,**" Stump said. "**My finest creation.**"

"See, **that's what I don't get,**" Kolb said. "All this new stuff . . . it doesn't make **any sense.**"

"What do you mean?" Stump asked.

"**Well . . .**"

Kolb went on to explain that the **game server, Aetheria,** was drastically **different** from normal Minecraft.

Minecraft had changed a lot since it was first created—**thirty years and still going strong**—yet, the Aetheria server ran a **mod,** which further **altered the game's rules.**

Stormberries were one of the countless new things **the mod** included. They grew on leaf blocks arranged to resemble bushes. And these **blue** and **yellow berries** could be used to craft a variety of different food items: stormberry cookies, stormberry tea, stormberry rolls and biscuits. . . .

"But **not cakes,**" he said. "That crafting recipe just **wasn't in** the game's **code.** Someone had suggested it on the forums once, but **Entity** never **programmed it in.** Some of us figure that whatever happened during the event not only trapped us inside but also somehow unlocked **a beta version** of the server. **A new update** that Entity **was working on.**"

"You've lost me," Max said. "All right, forget all that. What about you being a **Savior?**"

Kolb took a **deep breath.** "Entity added these things called **quests.** Like, you talk to a villager, and the villager asks you to fetch him some lava or something. **Boom,** you're on **a quest.** So you go scoop up some lava in a bucket, give it to the villager, and he gives you **a reward of some kind,** and the server rewards you with **experience points,** and the quest is complete. Right, anyway, **um,** I guess I was given **a special quest.** Quests come in **three different types.** First, there's your **ordinary quest.** Simple ones like fetching a villager something. Then there are **quest chains.** You complete one quest, it leads to another, which leads to another. Finally, you have **quest trees.** They're more **complicated,** nonlinear. Me being **a Savior** is all part of one **big quest tree.**"

"And what are you supposed to do?" I asked.

"I have to re-forge **this.**"

He pulled out **a sword** from his inventory. **Its blade seemed to be broken.**

Critbringer

(Keep in mind my poor drawing skill. These paws, you see. His sword looked way cooler than this.)

"I recognize **that metal**," Max said. "That **rainbow** effect . . . that's **adamant,** isn't it?"

"Yeah. This is **Critbringer,** one of the **swords** crafted by **Entity** thousands of years ago. He **gave it to me** in-game before everything went black, said it was **one of the most powerful** quest items **ever made.**"

Stump didn't seem too **impressed**: "If it's **so powerful,** why is it **broken?**"

"It's just part of the **lore.** Entity wrote **detailed history** for the server. According to **the story, Herobrine** tried to **destroy** the blade during **the Second War.** Now, **seven fragments** are supposedly scattered across the world. Shards, they're called. Upon finding one, I can forge it back into the blade by **re-crafting** it. Each shard added will slightly upgrade **the sword's abilities.** Damage and on-hit effects, attack speed, **all that.** The problem is **locating the pieces.**"

"**I saw one!**" I blurted out. "A few days ago. In the Nether."

I told him about **Rarg** and how he had taken **EnderStar's secret treasure horde.**

The human listened intently. "I have to say, I've been too **preoccupied** with the events here. Perhaps I'll pay them **a little visit?**"

Max opened the huge tome again. "You mentioned something about Herobrine trying to **destroy the sword.** Look. It's all right here in this book."

"That's the **lore.**" Kolb moved over and flipped through the pages. "**But it isn't complete.** The full lore is over **one thousand pages long. Entity** wrote this stuff over two years ago. When he became too busy with **programming,** he appointed several players as **scribes** to keep adding to the story."

"But you said Entity **crafted** that sword thousands of years ago," Stump said.

"**Right.** After the event, it's almost like whatever was written down in the lore **became reality** here."

(Um. Wow. Whenever I **level-up,** I really need to put more points into **Higher Intelligence,** because I don't understand much of anything.)

As far as I can grasp:

There was a **virtual reality** game on Earth known as **Minecraft.**

The world was **coming to an end,** so Kolb retreated into the game to say goodbye to his friends.

As their final hour approached, **the event** took place—everyone in the game blacked out and woke up here, and the game mysteriously came to life?

I glanced at the stormberry cake. "**Can I eat now?**"

"Sure." Stump handed me a slice. "**Nothing better** than home-crafted food."

After a cautious **sniff,** I ate the slice in a single bite—and promptly **spit out** crumbs. "Is . . . that . . . really . . . **food?!**"

That was Stump's **tipping point.** He was already in a **bad mood** after I devoured half a stack of his sugar *(sugar he crafted using his mom's special recipe, a family secret passed down through the generations)*, but **insulting** his **crafting** like that? It was almost as if he was a creeper in a villager costume **ready** to **explode.**

This morning, a boy named **Bumbi** taught me **how to build.**

At least, I think.

My goal was to build **a chicken house** behind the school. *(I think it's called a "chicken coop," but Bumbi kept saying "chicken house.")*

> It went okay at first.
> He gave me some oak blocks.
> I placed some oak blocks.
> It really did go okay.

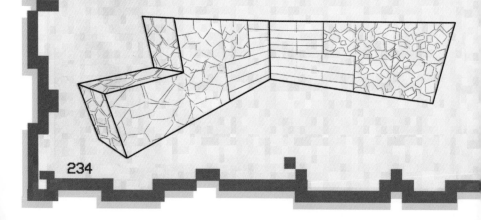

Then he **stopped** giving me oak blocks. Because he ran out. *(Is he really a teacher? Shouldn't a teacher be more prepared?)* Luckily, he had some **cobblestone.**

When he ran out of that, he gave me some **gravel**. When he ran out of that, he gave me some **pumpkins.**

And melons.

I'm no expert, but I'm fairly sure this guy didn't know what he was doing.

In Bumbi's world, this is what a chicken house is made of.

235

Since he had no more materials left to give me, he decided that I should use sand for the roof. That didn't work out so well.

Oak stairs are **much better** for roof building, he said. And when you run out of stairs, **well . . .** you'd better use fence. **Yeah, that's it.**

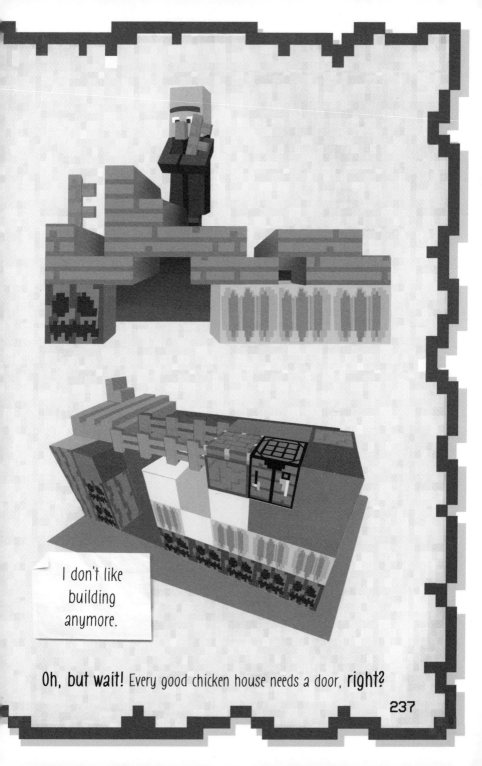

I don't like building anymore.

Oh, but wait! Every good chicken house needs a door, **right?**

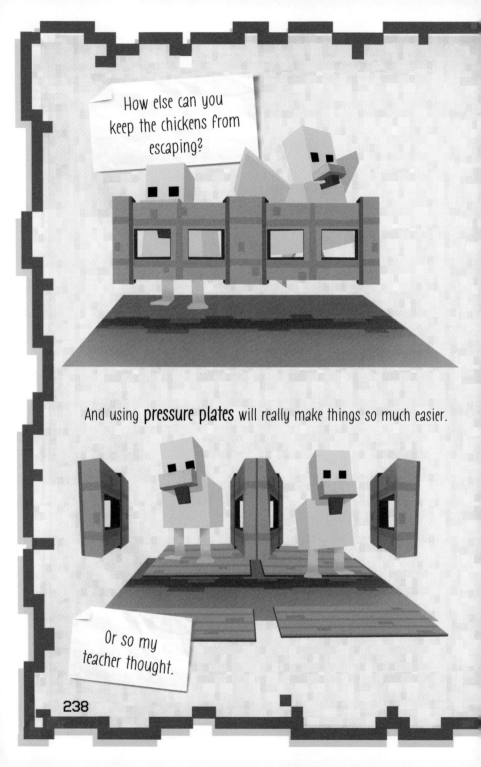

Later on today, I caught up with **Breeze** again.

She could sense that **something** was wrong. She kept asking me what was **on my mind.**

And she knew that it was more than just that **horrible** building experience with Bumbi. She knew it was something **serious.**

I wanted to tell her about what I'd learned yesterday with **Kolb,** but **I'd promised** not to say anything. Are we really living in **a game?** Am I just one of its **characters?**

If I really am just a so-called **NPC,** how am I able to **think** and feel . . . ?

And what about my **memories?** My past life? Endless days just being a **playful kitten**—are all of those memories **false?**

I'm **determined** to learn more about **my existence.** I want to know who I am. **What I am.** There must be a reason for all of this. **For this** world. **For me.**

And suddenly I recalled what **Rarg** had said to me. Sometimes, **he doesn't feel real.** I feel the same way when I'm **tired** or **stressed out.** Could it really be that I'm nothing more **than . . . ?**

"It's nothing," I said. "Just had a . . . **bad day.**"

"You sure?"

"Yeah."

As we wandered through the streets, I noticed that strange old man again. **Korbius.**

Breeze spotted him, too. It was pretty hard **not** to, honestly. He was just ten blocks away, **hiding behind some flowers.**

Breeze swiftly moved up to the rosebushes. "Why are you **spying** on us?"

The man stepped back, **flustered.** "What? **Me? Spying** on you?! Why no, I was simply . . . **admiring these flowers!** Yes! I **love flowers!** I'm a real connoisseur!"

"**Oh?** Then tell me: What color is **owl's eye?**"

"Well, **hmm . . .** I don't believe I've ever heard of such a flower. Could it be that I've met someone **more knowledgeable** about flowers than even myself? I find that **hard to believe!**"

"Just tell us why you keep **following us,**" Breeze said. "I saw you at the school. **The Clothing Castle,** too."

*(Really? She must have fantastic eyesight, because I didn't see him then. Although I did get the feeling that someone **was** watching us.)*

"Merely a **coincidence**," he said. "After all, I **am** a traveling merchant. **I'm always moving around!**"

"Whatever. See you around."

When she said this, **Korbius** smiled and said, "Oh, **yes.** I **will** be seeing you again. **Count on it.**"

Breeze stared at him for a moment, then turned to me. "Come on. **Let's go.**"

"**What's with** that guy?" I asked. "Was he really following us?"

"Yes. **Listen,** I need to go speak with my father. Maybe you can go have a **rest** now that your training is complete. See you back at the house?"

"Okay."

"By the way," she said, "my father agreed to let me **adopt you.**"

"**Adopt?** What is that?"

"It means my house is **your house** now."

"Forever?"

She smiled. "**Forever.**"

Last night, I had **horrible** nightmares.

I kept dreaming about what that human had said.

And **Runt.** When will I meet him? **What will happen** once I do?

I woke up in the middle of the night and **tossed and turned** on the carpet of Breeze's room. She was **stirring in her bed,** perhaps having **nightmares** as well.

I'm not sure why, **but . . .** I tried using **the tellstone** again. When I did, a variety of images flashed across the crystal's surface, from many different people, in many different places.

"Look at all these diamonds! They're everywhere!"

"Forget the diamonds for now! Look! See that vein?"

"Yeah. **WOW,** it's . . . what is that, five?"

243

"Attempt 61,785. Must. Discover. New. Crafting. Recipe. For. Master. Steve."

"Crafterbot attempting to craft. Failure. No new recipe discovered. Master Steve, when will you return . . . ?"

"I've lost track of how long I've spent in this reality. And I have yet to see Kolb."
—Ione

"Human, sir? We've taken you far enough. You really don't want to go beyond the river."

"Is that biome really haunted?"

"Papa thinks so. Things grow strangely there. The animals act funny. And then . . ."

"Exploring the Overworld is way more fun than tinkering around with redstone circuits all day!"

"Private Lola, reporting for duty!"

"Are we really
just NPCs . . . ?"

ABOUT THE AUTHOR

Cube Kid is the pen name of Erik Gunnar Taylor, a writer who has lived in Alaska his whole life. A big fan of video games—especially Minecraft—he discovered early that he also had a passion for writing fan fiction. Cube Kid's unofficial Minecraft fan fiction series, *Diary of a Wimpy Villager*, came out as e-books in 2015 and immediately met with great success in the Minecraft community. They were published in France by 404 éditions in paperback and now return in this same format to Cube Kid's native country under the title *Diary of an 8-Bit Warrior*. When not writing, Cube Kid likes to travel, putter with his car, devour fan fiction, and play his favorite video game.